Dr. Radway's
Sarsaparilla Resolvent

Dr. Radway's
Sarsaparilla Resolvent

by Beth Kephart
illustrated by William Sulit

New City Community Press
www.newcitycommunitypress.com

ISBN: 978-0-9840429-6-8

www.newcitycommunitypress.com

Cover design by William Sulit

Designed by Elizabeth Parks

3 1703 00575 0700

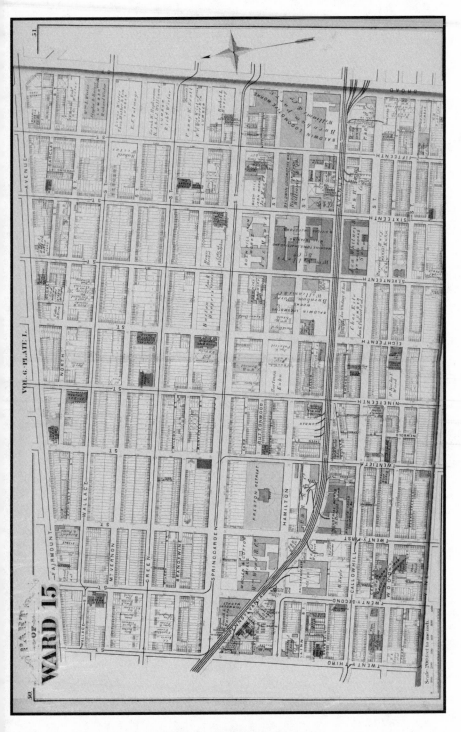

Dr. Radway's Sarsaparilla Resolvent

by Beth Kephart
illustrated by William Sulit

One

There was a story Francis told about two best friends gone swimming, round about Beiderman's Point, back of Petty's Island, along the crooked Delaware. "Fred Spowhouse," he'd say, his breath smelling like oysters and hay. "Alfred Edwards." The two friends found drowned and buckled together, Spowhouse clutched up tight inside Edwards's feckless arms.

It would practically kill Francis, every time he told the tale—the way the one died trying to put the rescue on the other. Francis would say it was the worst thing possible, the worst story told, but Francis didn't know the half of it. Worst thing possible was what happened to Francis six months later, and how it happened to Francis all alone.

Two

"I keep losing things," Ma says to William. The room is swampy, the shadows smug. A bottle of Bitter Wine of Iron sits lidless on the near table, a sorry spoon beside it. William wipes his forehead with his sleeve and studies the single mourning dove that will not leave the sill.

"Ma," he reminds her. "I'm still right here."

He stands up from the chair where he's been sitting. Measures the Bitter Wine onto the spoon while the dove watches with the flat disk of its eye. William worries briefly for the dove's mate, disappeared on the same day that he and Ma lost Francis. The one dove staying and the other dove gone, and William's mother dying by inches of heartache.

"Take your medicine, Ma," he says. "Doctor made you promise."

Nothing.

"Rejuvenation, Ma. Comfort. Says it right here on the label."

Ma turns. She closes her eyes and leaves William standing with the thick drip of the stuff on the spoon—E.F. Kunkel's Bitter Wine, bought with Francis's stealings for a hard one dollar. Lifting the spoon to his own mouth, William sucks it clean, then pours himself a foul second. The mourning dove cocks its head in a sideways scold.

"Mind your own," William tells it, but the bird just stares. Everything that's broken is William Quinn's to fix.

Three

William, fourteen years old and with his own heart broken, closes his eyes and thinks of Francis. The bloom of a bruise on the shin beneath his older brother's knee. A lump of butter in his pocket. Stolen things. That smile that never straightened itself. Those words he'd say about being lucky. Francis was a small-time thief. He was a charmer.

We're lucky people, William.

We're not hardly lucky, Francis.

It's still a hot day, a long day. It's Ma not stirring in her bed, and Kunkel's medicine like a first-class sham, and that bird waiting on William to do something. *Be* something. *You aren't any kind of man,* the bird thinks. William almost says it.

"Ma," William says instead. "Listen, Ma. Francis wouldn't like you lying here. You know how Francis is."

"*Was*, William. Francis *was*. Everything I had is gone."

Everything. There it is again. As if William doesn't know. As if he wasn't the first Quinn to get the news: *Your brother's been murdered for trespass.* It was Mrs. May next door who came knocking furious on the door and who broke in fast when the answer didn't come, and who stood there in the place a parlor would be in a bigger house, crazy with her telling, sure of her story because Rebecca Harberger had told it to her—the truth and the hearsay.

Francis Quinn, William's one fine brother, had been found by the sound of his snoring in somebody else's shed, some time nearing 5 A.M., the drink he favored having gone to his head. Officer Socrates F. Kernon on his early shift was the one who pulled Francis clean of the shed by the scruff of his neck—yanked him, even as Francis was still sleeping.

I'm sorry, sir, for the trespass. Mrs. May saying that that's what Francis said, when he was awake enough for the protest. *Don't hit me—, you'll fetch back the hemorrhage on me.*

But Officer Kernon was a monster, spit-shined mean, and as Mrs. May told the tale, Ma stood there, frozen. Halfway down the steps and halfway up them, William catching her so she wouldn't fall.

Some of the murdering happened in an alley and some of it happened in the street. All of it happened as the dawn became day, as the birds started to stir, as Francis's last night of drink wore itself off.

I've done nothing, Francis was heard saying, and that's when, according to Mrs. May, Officer Kernon put the nippers on and hauled Francis past a cow gone wrong, past people staring, past an old lady in a night dress, past two young men shouting, toward the police station. That's how Mrs. May told it: Francis dragged the whole way, kicking and pleading, dragged there until he was dead. The coroner was the one who had suspected the blackjack. No nose or head comes in ruined like that, without the use of blackjack.

What have they done to my Francis? Ma said. She'd fallen completely into William by now. She was thin and bone white shaking, and she couldn't understand; she wouldn't. She told the story again as questions. Her words came out like whispers.

Murdered for trespass.

Trespass?

Split him ripe with a blackjack.

Who did?

Officer Kernon.

Officer murdered our own Francis? For trespass?

Man has the face of an octopus.

It's been weeks. It's been long enough for Ma's own disappearing, into the shadows and heat. William stands up tall. He leaves the dark for the sun, the house for the street, the cowering he's been doing for the strength he'll need to find the murderer who didn't take Francis only, but stole Ma's treasured thing. It's up to William now.

"Ma," he says. "I'll be back."

She turns her spine to him.

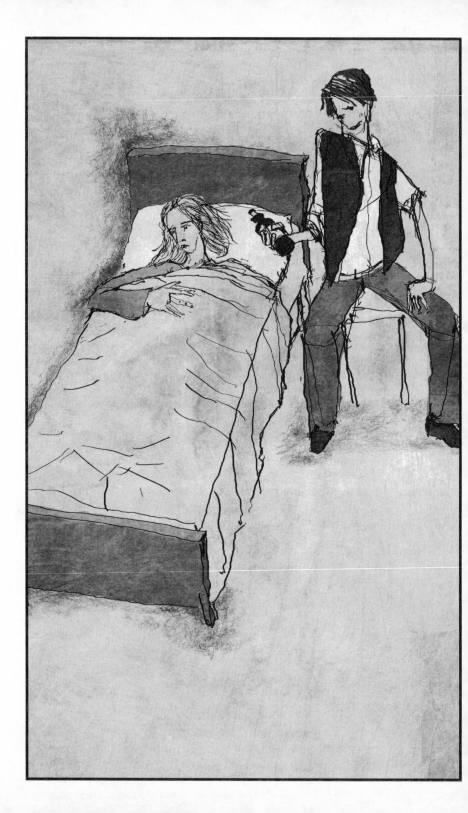

Four

The sound of the machines comes down around him: the lathing and whining and huffing and steaming of the manufactories of old Bush Hill. It's a bee-in-the-ear sound—the infernal song of warp split and hank twist, beam and grist, the raking in of steaming coal, the mash and heat of pig iron. Corner to corner, at every careen and cross, it's here: the Iron Works, the Tool Works, the Car-Wheel Works, the plundering shake of the Pennsylvania Railroad, the stones being knocked from the trench.

William lives where the new world is made, in the heart of progress. He turns from Carleton at Twenty-first and then heads east along the railroad tracks on Pennsylvania Avenue toward the acres of brick and glass, the stacking of chimneys, the black stripes of pluming smoke above Baldwin's locomotive yard.

Monster of a man.

Face like an octopus.

A stick up his sleeve, like a black finger.

William's on the hunt for Kernon.

"Watch it, boy," someone calls out from behind, and through the heat and the dust, William sees a train coming—a P&R headed for the depot at Callowhill, with its seven-cent commuters catching a bit of open air. It's the machinist crowd from the north and east—the flangers, fitters, riveters, carters, chippers, caulkers coming in, their laundered aprons tucked up beneath one arm. Pa should be here, would be here, if he weren't locked up at Cherry Hill.

I'll get him free, Francis used to say.

And Ma would believe him, because she'd believe anything Francis said, even though nobody gets free from Cherry Hill.

There'll be a breakout, Francis used to say. *You'll see.*

Can't be done, Career would tell him. *Impossible.*

Somebody someday will find a way, Francis would say. *I bet my good luck on it.*

A bell clangs. A horse pulled over on the street grows nervous in front of its cab. The noise is harder here. The heat bangs under the intemperate sovereignty of the countless machines. *I'm coming for you,* William thinks. *I'm coming for what is rightfully the Quinns'.*

But the morning is fierce and fast, and if Kernon's here in all of this, how is William supposed to find him? If Kernon's come, he's lurking, casting mean suspicions on the crowd.

William fits his hand over his brow to block the sun. He hurries and he stops. He leans against a long wall of brick and watches—across the tracks, through the dust, between the horses and the cabs—as the piece workers come, the draftsmen, the foremen, the managers in their shined black boots. All of these people to watch and measure. All of these strangers, none Kernon. An old man in a winter's coat stands perfectly

10

still, a beard just past his chin, the morning *Inquirer* in his hands. DEATH ON THE RAIL, the headline screams. APPALLING SCENES AND MIRACULOUS ESCAPES. There's a tear, William notices, in the old man's rheumy eye.

"What do you want, boy?" the man asks, looking up suddenly and dropping the news at his feet, like he's embarrassed to be seen caring about other people's hurting. He gives William one last look then walks into the crowds—pushes his way into the surge until he vanishes like smoke.

William watches him go, then bends and scoops the paper off the street. He folds it quick and stuffs it into his belt against his skin, then tucks his chin and heads east, with the crowds, east into the noise, looking still for Kernon. He'll walk until his feet hurt and the news is scratchy on his skin. He'll walk until he hardly hears the noise and barely notices the stray pup at his feet, latched on like something familiar. He'll walk until the trains run the reverse, and the crowds swamp back on him, until it is time, he knows it, to go home.

And he'll see no one with a monster face. No one with a stick up his sleeve, a thick black finger.

Five

The dove's on the sill. Ma's tragic in her bed and also in her mirror—its rumpled, freckled glass doubling the small box of the room.

"You think Alburger's Celebrated German Bitters could do you right?" William asks Ma now. He's at her side. He's said nothing of his dusty walk, the way he turned sometimes, just to see if Francis were walking beside him. He reads the old man's paper, with the scenes and the escapes—the advertisements between all the stories.

"You think the bitters can bring back Francis?" Ma says.

"Ad says it's Celebrated," William says, leaning in, smoothing the hair from Ma's face. "Ad says nothing about Francis." It's five in the afternoon, and the heat has settled in with the gray sheets, the bent spoon, the E.F. Kunkel's. There's a pair of shoes by the side of the bed that sweats along the buckles.

"Francis is missing," Ma says.

"I know it, Ma."

"There's nothing for it."

"How about Dr. Van Dyke's?" William says, reading the promises of another medicine ad. "Could it soothe you, Ma? Do you think?"

She doesn't say.

"I'm going to cut you some rye, Ma. Dress it with jam."

"My throat won't take it."

"Your throat?"

"Can't swallow."

"I'll make you some tea," William says. "It'll help."

He reaches in, lifts Ma into his arms. He presses a kiss to her forehead then straightens to find the balance of her, catching the sight of them both in the mirror across the room—William sandy-haired and river-eyed, Ma rubbed away and sinking, the two of them together like a lowercase T. Ma's hair is yellow and loose, a curl fallen to the center of her forehead. Her skin is pale, her hands just slightly blue. She doesn't weigh her right size. She doesn't resist. When the sheet pulls away, her nightdress bunches at her knees. It's Ma's feet that frighten William most of all—the color of bone and much too skinny to put any walking on.

"What's going to happen, William?" she asks. They're taking the stairs, one step at a time. William tucks in his elbows and turns to the side, careful not to knock Ma's head, to keep her feet from breaking.

"One thing," he tells her, measuring his words, "at a time." He pauses at the final step, then takes the few paces to the kitchen, where four weary cane-bottomed chairs are pulled around the table. He fits her down onto the sturdiest. She sinks, catches her head with her blue hands.

"Making you tea, Ma."

Nothing.

"Making you rye with marmalade." Outside, in the street, the Harbergers are playing—all seven of them—including Molly, who screams over the spray of the hydrant until Mrs. May leans out the crack of her window and tells them each to civilize. At the table, Ma doesn't so much as flinch.

"Ma," William finally confesses. "I'm going to make things right. I will."

She doesn't hear him, maybe. Or she doesn't believe.

With the back of his finger, he spreads marmalade on the rye. Into Ma's cracked cup he pours the tea, which is hot water mostly, a little taint of yellow to it. Over the ascendant tea, Ma watches.

"Don't make promises you can't keep," she says, at last.

"I don't."

"It's not you that I'm not trusting, William. It's the rest of everything. Our luck so bad."

He slides the cup of tea beside Ma's elbow. He tucks his hand beneath her chin, and lifts, but she resists, her unwillingness the strongest thing about her.

"You drink some," he says. "Let me see it."

She gives him a hard, glancing look, then obeys him. Briefly.

"All right," he says. "One more sip. At least." Knowing in his heart that Ma drinking tea fixes nothing.

He wants to say, *I failed*.

He wants to tell her that his heart's broke, too.

But a real man keeps his suffering to himself, and so he says nothing.

He waits.

He lets the hour grow so silent that Ma lifts her head then and looks *into* him, like it's the first time she's seen him in days. Like he's only just there, her one not-lost thing, with the marmaladed day-old and tea the color of Bush Hill rainwater. Sadness appears in the corner of Ma's eye. It slowly finds her chin.

Six

The dove is still there as the sun starts its slide. Ma is back in her bed, but not sleeping. The mirror is doubling the size of the room and smudging to blackness the gray.

"Take the tea with you, Ma," William had said downstairs, when they were still in the kitchen. "At least."

"Tomorrow," she had told him. "Tomorrow, I'll have some more."

There was no arguing with her. He'd carried her back up those steps, like an empty dress in his arms. Had taken his place in the chair beside the bed and was half asleep when he heard the knock on the front door.

"Coming!" he'd called out.

Then, to his Ma, he'd whispered, "That'll be Career."

He'd pulled on a pair of Francis's trousers, belted up, checked the pockets, and found a chip of coal that Francis must have tucked away after a day of hunting the line; he'd slipped it under the bed for later. He'd taken the stairs quick, grabbed his cap. He'd opened the door to his best friend, who leaned hard into the brick and held a match to the end of a pipe, his head cocked toward the dying sounds of the power looms being tooled across the street. Career wore his charcoal-colored sack jacket and his one too-big-for-him vest. The dust had been rubbed from the crease in his boots.

The two set off down Carleton, stepping through the pool of the hydrant's wasted water and giving a nod to Mrs. May, leaning out her window—nosy as always and putting a gloss on the hairs of her chin.

"Your Ma all right?" Mrs. May calls.

"Had some rye," William says. "Some tea."

"You keep at it boy, you hear me?"

Her voice sounding like bad news, always, no matter how nice she tries to be.

Career wears his black hair long, past his ears. William wears his tucked inside his cap. Career walks straight, to make himself taller. William, tall, walks a crouch. More hydrants have gone off up and down—the spurt and the fizzle of water, free. The flangers, the fitters, the chippers, and caulkers are home. The patternmakers and carpenters. The iron molders and turners. The ones who make the boilers go. The casting cleaners and assistants. Not Pa. It's visiting hours up at the penitentiary. Career always comes along.

The boys cross the tracks and make their way up past Hamilton and Preston Retreat through the sound of fussing babies and the worrying or wanting of their new mothers. Two men rolling a lopsided barrel pass, the barrel making its own kind of song. William stops for a moment in the Preston garden shade. Closes his eyes to smell the drift of summer flowers. Opens his eyes and still says nothing. It's wicked in Bush Hill in summer.

"You all right?" Career asks.

"How could I be all right?" William says.

Career doesn't answer. Career's been a song seller, an organ grinder, a crockery king, a blackener, a boy running soup from the almshouse to the ladies in need, protecting their reputation for a penny a bowl. Now Career runs messages for Mr. Childs' *Public Ledger* and keeps his wages in a buried can. Saving up, he says, for the One Thing.

"What's the One Thing?" William will ask him.

Career never says. Career won't.

"Come on," Career says. "Your Pa's waiting." He pulls a stone out of his trouser pocket, drops it to the street, and kicks it ahead to William, who leaves the shade of Preston Retreat and smacks the stone crosswise and up. Two twin girls in dresses like pink parasols pass by, their mother stern in blue. Career looks up, winks, then lopes, knocking the stone to where William would be if he wasn't still staring at the girls, both with identical ginger hair and jewel eyes—neither, somehow, like the other. Neither, mostly, like the mother, who casts her opinion on William and hurries her procession along.

William feels the heat in his face and runs for the stone. He smacks it hard Career's way. The game stays good between them now—past Spring Garden and Brandywine, Green, Mt. Vernon, Wallace, all the way to Cherry Hill, where finally they stop and stand in the long skirt of the prison's shadows, its massive gothic gloom. Cherry Hill runs the full block and back, two hundred feet in the east-west direction, four crenellated towers on its front face and a watchman high, looking for trouble. Career works a match into the shallow bowl of his pipe, and it takes. The tobacco flares sweet. The two boys stand in the shadow of the prison. Visiting hours. End of day. The guards in their towers, watching.

"You going to call to him, then?" Career asks, after a while.

"Those walls so damned thick."

"You going to try it anyway?"

"Your whistling," William says. "It works better."

Career blows the smoke of his pipe through the spaces between his teeth. He finds his song, and it carries. William closes his eyes and imagines his Pa inside — past the vaulted doors and the iron gates, beneath the eye of the warden and of God. People are puny at Cherry Hill. People are locked away to consider what they've done.

"You think he can hear that?" Career asks, stopping his song.

"Keep on."

Career picks the song back up, and William stands there in the shadows, at his best friend's side, trying to see Pa in his mind's eye, trying not to remember the last time he saw his father free. "Don't do it, Pa," Francis had warned him. Ma, too. *Don't, don't, don't.*

But it had happened.

It was too late.

Now Pa is here in lock-up, Cherry Hill silent as a vault, and William is trying to remember the last time Pa was happy. Nobody breaks free of Cherry Hill.

Career whistles a professional melody. It carries high and sweet and maybe Pa is listening, maybe he is. William hears what he thinks is the wind, but it's a bird winging in close, that dove from the sill tucking its wings then letting them go, its rise effortless. Career stops his song and looks up. The bird goes on, north and west—a free line across the prison wall and out, toward the river.

"That's my dove," William says.

"You have a dove now?"

"Suppose I do."

"You all right?" Career asks again.

"Can't say I am," William says. "Can't say it and be truthful."

"You can't stay in all day," Career says. "It's helping no one."

"I don't."

"You don't?"

"Today I was on the hunt for Kernon."

"Kernon the officer?"

"That's the one."

"How you going to find him?"

"By looking."

"That won't work."

"You have other ideas?"

Career leans his head back, closes his eyes, and thinks, the thinking all over his face. "How about Norris House?"

"Why Norris House?"

"Isn't that where all the nasties go?'

"Maybe."

"Isn't Kernon a nasty?"

"Big time, he is."

"Maybe Kernon goes to Norris House. Specific is better than general. That's what the say all the time, in the news."

"Maybe," William says.

"Maybe?"

"Do another tune," William says. "For my Pa."

"Think about it," Career says. "Think what Francis would do."

Francis ginned up or Francis sober? There's a difference, and Career knows it, too. It's hard to be sure of what Francis would do. It's hard to think of going off to Norris.

"Pa's waiting for your song," William says at last.

"All right."

"Make it a nice one."

"I do."

Career O's up his mouth and whistles a tune. He makes it pretty and high.

Seven

It's gone to dark. Career's out of song. They've called out, both of them, across the thick prison wall.

"Night, Pa."

"Night, Mr. Quinn."

Together they've walked the streets, passed Preston Retreat, looked for the twins, couldn't find them. At the corner of Callowhill, Career set off for his own home. He'll be at the old *Public Ledger* by six tomorrow, hoping for a one-on-one with Mr. George Childs, the *Ledger's* leader. Career calls it his up-and-coming. He talks of it sometimes, when he thinks that William has room for something more than troubles.

"You think Childs will talk to you? Actual talk?" William will ask.

"George Childs is a talent appreciator," Career will say, with a smile. "And I've got talent."

"What do you want from Mr. Childs?" William will say, when they talk of it—when they forget, for a while, the unlucky Quinns.

"I want him to take me serious," Career will answer. "I want him to see where I am going. Make me a reporter. Trust me with news."

It's a long shot dream. It's Career, who named himself.

Now at his mother's bedside, William sits thinking. He sits remembering Francis and all that he was, trying to figure himself into his

older brother's shoes. Man with an octopus face: How would Francis net him? Man with a black finger: What would Francis do to subdue? How would Francis force a confession? How would he finagle back the second thing the monster cop stole? Not just Francis's life, which is enough. Cop took more of the Quinns than that, even.

Francis? William says. Almost. *Francis, where are you? I need you.*

William sits in the hot dark, thinking. He sits there, but all that comes is memories of Francis carrying fresh bird home for Ma to cook, Francis waltzing through the house like the house was big, Francis making William read the news to him, Francis teaching William things about the river.

Would you go to Norris House looking? William wants to ask his brother. *Would you?* He needs his brother's advice. He needs to know what's best and smartest. But all William gets in his mind's eye is October, near a year ago, when the single scullers are racing the river, and Francis is keen on Max Schmitt.

"Little brother," Francis is saying, as William remembers. "We're going."

I don't have time to remember, William almost says. But he gives in, he always did, to Francis.

The knees of the ghost Francis are bent. The shoulders are stooped. The wild hair is pushed to one side and pinched with yellow sticks of straw. Francis snatches William's trousers from the hook on the door and sends them on a short fly across the room, and William can feel this now, can feel the smack of the trousers as they hit his bare chest, can feel the tug of them up his own bony legs as he scrambles to chase Francis out the door and down the stairs. It's William who stops to write the note for Ma, since Francis is no speller. They carry their boots outside and lace up on the stoop. Francis pokes at his hair with his hands, William tucks in his nightshirt, and they're walking.

The race will be run above the dam, in the stilled part of the Schuylkill that some around town call a lake. It will run itself north, collecting near Turtle Rock, scooping past a minor island and around a bend, spectators gathering on either shore and on the bridges above, until the scullers reach the stake beneath the Columbia Railroad Bridge and turn downriver. Francis is hurrying William into a run, past a game of penny toss, between the ladies carrying their laundry loads, past the taverns, where some men still sit, dazed and haloed by the morning sun.

It's not until they work their way around the reservoir and reach the east bank of the river that Francis slows and runs his long, bony fingers through his mopped, brown hair. He walks with a bit of a bow in his back, his feet drawing themselves into a V.

"Wouldn't Pa be loving this though?" Francis calls to William, who is catching his breath from behind.

"Would be."

Francis squats on the flint of a rock and pulls his lanky legs to his chin; William sinks, too. They search for blades of grass to chew and look out across the painted boathouses of the Schuylkill's eastern shore, the glisten of the Water Works that paddles the river out of itself and up, toward the reservoir of Faire Mount and then out through the hollow pipes that snake beneath the city, invisible.

"You see Schmitt?" William asks.

"Not yet."

"You tell me when you do?"

"You'll know him," Francis says. "When he comes through."

They let time go. They wait until Francis is ready to rise, until the true, blue shade is gone from beneath the hemlock and pine and the crowds have swelled. William stands when Francis stands, and they make their way past the gaping doors of the boathouses, stealing their long looks at the sculls and the crews and the contraptions inside before they climb higher into the carved paths of The Hills. They cross over footbridges, over stone, between prickly patches of laurel and rhododendron, never taking their eyes from the Schuylkill. There's a painter setting his easel up, boxes of paint at his feet.

The sky is ripe blue. The clouds are smoke puff. The day's headed for gold; William feels it. All around them, the people come, choose their looking places. A German band plays some song.

"You think Schmitt'll take it, Francis?"

"I know he will."

"Brossman's beat him before."

"That was the four-mile, '68. Today's the three."

Three miles in the single sculls. Three miles of scull speed and oar dig, the haul of narrow boats through a river and after a while of waiting and speculating, of watching the crowds come in and thicken, a pistol sends the boats into their race.

The crowd is on its feet—the hats and the veils and the kerchiefs like flags in their hands. William fits his hand over his eyes to block the sun and looks to the tugs behind the rope lines, the crowds along the bridge, the carriages that have pulled up short along the river's west bank. There's not an empty back of granite in the cliffs, not an empty square in the stands, and when the holler goes out, Francis leans in close.

"Schmitt's got the lead," he says.

The sculls cut the river's blue. They turn the bend, and the roar builds; the roar is a mighty wallop of sound as Schmitt and Street and Brossman and Lavens dig the river hard—Schmitt ahead and every single person yelling, every hand pumping the flag of something white or red or yellow or blue, so that it seems to William that an entire nation of birds has swooped in and is testing its plentiful wings. Francis yells loud as the best of them. He throws his broad, white hand to the sky, like the finest bird of all, and beneath the Girard Avenue Bridge, Brossman and Street mangle their oars into each other's, and the crowd calls out, "Foul! Foul!"

"Three lengths ahead!" Francis shouts, and it's Schmitt all the way, after the turn, Schmitt with his scull three lengths ahead, and Francis taking off for the finish line, running with the crowd, and William running, too, his eye on the river. Schmitt is steady in the lead. He's steady, and nobody takes his eyes from him—even the Germans have stopped playing and a spilled pot of paint is running down the hill.

"Our one for the books," Francis is shouting, over his shoulder, still running, still electric with Schmitt's 20-minute river run, and the blue in the sky and the gold that did come on, that is. The hero wins. The hero is Schmitt, and it is also Francis, running, his hair mopping all around his head, his whole long, lanky self blazing bright with living. Francis alive and running, and suddenly William is certain: Francis would be the hero, if he could. Francis would go to Norris House. Francis would stand up and leave the dark. He'd go out there, take his chances.

"All right," William says. "You win, big brother."

Eight

William waits until nine that night, then slips away. Down the narrow sleeve of the stairs and through the heavy shadows of the room and out into the street and down toward Nelson. He takes nothing with him but a knife, for caution. He feels the rumble of nerves in his guts, looks around in the dark, wishes he had more of a plan than just getting up and going.

But that is his plan. Getting up and going.

He hears the clatter of something behind him and turns to find a loose hog scrambling toward him. He sees a man on the chase, a hackney carriage in the distance. Somebody's tune floats down from an open window, the faint sound of an argument. The closer William gets to the Norris House tavern, the more he's overcome by the sound of the streets, the smell of meat parts and heat, the aggravation and rot. He could still go back, but he knows he won't. Turning is for cowards, and maybe somewhere up there, Francis is watching.

"Out of the way, such as you can," someone yells at the corner of Broad and Callowhill. William hurries to the right, and then looks up, and there's the sign where it always is: Norris House. From inside comes the sound of pots flying, the sound of someone cursing a sweet streak.

There's a tightness in William's throat, like a gasket closing. There's the sharpness of nerves in his pocket, where the knife is. William opens the door and chooses a table to the left of things. Slips in, just like that, hoping no one sees. He studies the angles—the minor crowd at the bar, the one man at the front table, fast asleep, a newspaper like a tent over his head. Along the back wall a bar stretches end-to-end—a half height of worn-out wood—and beyond the bar itself sit a wide barrel of beer and a scattering of thin-necked bottles that catch the flares sent out by kerosene. A man is working the bottles, the beer; must be Old Murphy. From the runt of a room to the right, a heavy band of smoke lolls, the smell of crusted bread and grease, old fire. The thinnest man William's ever seen stands at the threshold, gauging business.

"One husband not enough for you, then, Pearl?" Old Murphy is saying to the blowzy reddish blonde on the barstool. She's got a man on either side and no air between—all three of them pale and stained, beads of sweat on their necks, as if the weather has affronted each in the same way.

"Neither of 'em worth a penny," this blowzy Pearl says, taking each of her companions in. Her voice is as low as a man's. William tries not to notice, but he does. He watches the door, then again watches Pearl. He fingers his knife, wonders how long Old Murphy will let him sit here, nothing on his table but his hands.

"Worth the weight of you in gold," one of Pearl's men is saying. "The weight of him, too." He reaches the long way around Pearl and jabs at his rival with a thumb.

"You're both nothing," Pearl tells them, crossing her arms across her chest, and losing her balance, for a moment, on the stool, though the men catch her—both of the men at the same time. At the other end of the bar a man with a face the color of sausage lets out a long, low whistle. He pulls a coin from his purse and splats it down, says he'd like to show the others how it is you treat a madam, and Old Murphy plants his elbows on the bar and leans his chin into his hands.

"Jerry, if you will," he says to the cook, "the lady wants oysters."

"Oysters and a pint of ale," Pearl corrects. She rolls a long, wild curl around her own hand and exhales real slow. The sausage-faced man sends his bright half-dollar for a long ride toward Old Murphy, who is still just leaning there.

"You buying for Thomas and Bryant, too?" Old Murphy asks, turning the coin over in his hand and looking to either side of the blowzy.

"Buying to please the madam," the sausage man says.

"Three bowls, three pints, and nothing short will please the madam."

"Four," Pearl says, turning suddenly on her stool and taking the glances of the four men with her. "One for the boy in the corner, who hasn't got none." William feels his face go hot.

"That'll be it, then?" Old Murphy asks, after taking a long, appraising look at William and back at Pearl. "Four of each?" Jerry disappears into the cave of his kitchen to get his business done.

William hears the crack of an egg against a pan, smells the infiltrating spice of cayenne pepper. He sees a cloud of fast-moving smoke and the man with the sausage face shaking his head—disgusted, happy—taking another coin from his purse and sending it down the slick length of the bar. Old Murphy mitts it, flips it, gives an approving nod. He chooses four mugs from a shelf above, wipes them clean with an apron corner, turns his attention to the barrel, and all this time William's watching the door, waiting for the arrival of his monster man, trying not to demonstrate his own enormous hunger.

Vigilance. That's what Career would say. Business first, then pleasure. Francis? Francis, William worries, would be asking for a rum. William is all William has right now. All there is.

The door opens and slams shut. The bottles of liquor along the back wall shuffle and clink, and the beer in the mug that Old Murphy's been filling sloshes over onto the bar. The man with the tent of news on his head turns and stares but it's not Kernon who has come in. It's that woman from the other day—the serious mother of the pink-parasol twins. She sets a sheaf of magazines on the short end of the bar and tells Jerry to give a copy each to every woman who comes in, tells Pearl herself to have a look.

"*The Revolution*," she says, naming the magazine and touching Pearl on the shoulder, like they're old friends, familiar. Pearl tips back her head and laughs, says she's not a reader, don't everybody know it? "You make yourself a reader, then," the woman says, like learning for a blowzy is so easy. Then the woman leaves like she came, in a high and purposeful rush. William watches her go and considers her daughters. Wonders if they're outside somewhere, their parasols raised to the moon.

"You hungry, Boy?" Old Murphy calls out to William, once the door to the tavern slams shut and Pearl is safe among her men.

William nods, feels the shame shoot through him.

"Tonight's your lucky night, then," Old Murphy says. "Looks like you found yourself a patron." He smiles at the man with a sausage face, revealing a bright gold tooth in a mouth full of holes. But there's no luck like the luck that William came here hunting. Two beers and a plate of oysters later, and Officer Kernon still doesn't show.

Nine

The next evening, Career's back leaning into the brick face of the Quinn row, wearing his same charcoal sack jacket, that cranberry-colored vest. His hair is parted slick. His boots have the day's dust on them. Molly, the Harberger youngest, is calling for a game of penny toss.

"Ask your brothers," Career calls back. "You've got enough."

Molly skips along like she hasn't heard, tugs at the hem of Career's jacket.

"What did I tell you?" Career says, stooping down, taking the girl's hands in his own, stern but not unkind.

"My brothers is off," Molly says. She lifts her hand out of Career's to the straggle of her hair and pushes it back behind both ears.

"You wait for them, then. I've got my business with William." He nods at his friend, standing there impatient.

"Can I come?"

"No, you cannot."

Molly crosses her arms and juts out her chin. "I hate being small," she declares.

Career reaches into his pocket and finds Molly a penny. "Can you keep a trust?" he asks.

She nods. "I can."

"Then you practice your toss with this penny, Molly, and I'll play you a game tomorrow."

Molly looks like she can't believe her luck. She swipes the penny from Career's palm, throws her head back and laughs, a goosing sound.

"Go on," Career says.

She spins on her toes, whirrs off. Career stands and knocks the dust from his knees, straightens his jacket and vest and walks, William matching him stride for stride.

William finds a stone, kicks it. Career runs ahead, not eager at first, contemplating something. They go for a distance before they talk again, and now it's William who's asking the questions.

"You have your up-and-coming with Mr. Childs?"

"I will."

"You so sure?"

Career nods, a quick flick of his head. He kicks the stone off toward the street's dirty margins and offers his defense—ticking down the facts of George Childs, the *Ledger* editor, a poor-to-rich bona fide. It's Career's good luck story, and he tells it as he wants, of how Childs—three dollars, no more, in his pocket—boarded a train for Philadelphia at a fatherless fourteen and found himself a sweeping and clerking spot at the Sixth and Arch bookstore. Four years more, and Childs was making and selling books of his own, soon enough buying himself a proper home near the Square—a big and fancy. Thomas Edison and Walt Whitman and Oscar Wilde and

Andrew Carnegie visit Childs on the Square, President Ulysses S. Grant, too. Career prowls the shadows, late at night, sees his country's history sliding by. "Pauper to prince," Career says, relating Childs' biography as if he were boasting on his own, as if the mere existence of the newspaper man makes any poor person's striving the most reasonable thing of all.

Career has worked messenger at the *Ledger* for four months now. Takes the back and forth from the reporters to the composers to the machines — going floor to floor and down, to the press room, where a massive Corliss drives the presses and the folding machines, and where the carriers wait, in a gallery balcony, for the news of the day to get made. "Industry," Career says, repeating on Childs. "Temperance. Frugality." The words that will take Career out of the life that is his into the life he's sure he was born for. "If a man has good principles and does his best to act up to them, he should not fail of success."

"You taking those principles to the bank?" Francis would ask, when it was the three of them on the long walk to Cherry Hill.

"You watch me," Career would say. "See how I do it."

But Francis isn't here, and William doesn't say it. William knows what Career knows, too: They're working on dreams, both of them.

"Coming on!" Career shouts, and in the nick of time only, William turns to see a goat with a rope coiled loose around its neck barreling from the east up Twenty-first. It's pure white and too loose on its legs — no more, William figures, than a month old, with its long ears flopping like a pair of socks.

38

"She's a runaway," Career says, and William agrees. She's skittish, and William looks past her toward three dogs on the chase, their tongues slashed crooked between the daggers of their teeth. The kid screams as her hooves slide on the stones. She knocks back up and runs a dazed, jagged line, while the dogs gain straight line speed.

William runs effortless, the way he does, the loose folds of Francis's trousers catching the wind and making a gentle slap, slap against William's thighs and shins. The dogs scud haunch to haunch—a gang, a stampede— and Career's running, too, drawing two of the dogs off on a diverting line and hollering for his own ambitious life. The biggest dog of the three veers William's way, and Career tacks back, his own two monster mutts yipping near to his feet. The kid scrambles. The third dog won't take its eyes, nor its speed, off of William.

"I got you," William's saying to the kid. "I got you." Talking soft and spreading his arms steady and wide. A couple of machine men come out onto their stoops, and behind them a couple of wives. Some boys stream out, too—middle-sized kids with battering sticks—until they're part of the storm wilding by. "I ain't going to hurt you," William is telling the kid, though the mutt that has not been diverted is readying itself to leap, its hackles high. All of a sudden, the kid stops, goes rock-solid still. Amidst the shout and the frenzy, the mania of dogs, the thundering appeals on the part of Career, the kid stands where she has stopped, pure white and knock-kneed and intransigent, the rope loose around her neck.

"Watch it!" Career shouts, and William does—eludes the barreling rise of the mutt and sweeps the kid into the net of his arms. The dog goes high onto its back heels, breathing its hot air into William's ear, its angry, salivating growl. The kid kicks and William feels the start of a bruise at his shoulder, his neck, the white bristle of the goat on his skin. William ducks and weaves, holding the bleating kid tight while a boy who has run in from behind beats the dog back with a stick, calling it by name as if the beast were a pet.

"You old coot," the boy says, and the dog falls to nothing, a whimper. Stands there with its hungry eyes while William, the kid suddenly yielding to his firm clutch, finds his cap, blown off in the wilding. He's turned south before Career has caught his pace.

"No Cherry Hill tonight," Career says, after a while, his words coming out between hard breaths.

"Tomorrow," William says. "We'll go." The kid startles at the sound of William's voice. William puts one hand to her head, strokes her calm, and the kid crooks his neck and licks William's chin.

"You think your Pa will miss us?"

"Maybe so." William pictures Pa, behind the gates, inside his cell, beneath the eye of the coming moon. Thinks about what Pa would do if he saw William headed home with a goat.

"I'll be needing me a seamstress," Career says, after they've walked together some.

"What for?"

Career lifts his arm to show William the place where the sleeve of his jacket has come loose from its seam. Career smiles, showing off his half an eyetooth.

"I'll ask Ma," William tells him, speaking softly. The goat has settled again.

"*Your* Ma?"

William doesn't answer him. The sun is low.

Ten

Career lights his pipe with a flame, then transfers the light to a window wick. The edge of the table is a ribbon of gray. The shadows are steep between the loose weaves of the caned chairs. Ma's big pots are dull glints hanging from the hooks on the wall, her stirring ladle and her soup pot, too. The cup of tea is cold. The flies on the rye are swelling. Dried husks of flowers pose in the long row of empty Nathan Brothers' Pine Apple Rye bottles along the floor—found, Francis would say, in his travels (though borrowed, William always suspected, from the ladies of Preston Retreat).

"You didn't steal from anybody's daisies, did you, Francis?" Ma would ask him.

"I wouldn't," he'd say, but he had.

Ma's big spinner sits with a round of yarn caught up in its bobbin, her satchel of sewing provisions at its side. She was working a pair of cuffs for Mrs. Spencer when Francis died, working them by hand. They sit where she left them, on the sill in the bare gray light.

"Your Ma will be surprised," Career says.

"She will."

"You going to keep her?"

William shrugs.

"You ever kept a goat before?"

"Not as I can remember."

"You'd remember that," Career says. "I'm pretty sure."

The kid brays, points with its tongue. She tastes the sweat on William's neck, the round platter of his top shirt button. "You behave now," William tells her, lowering her to the rough planks of the floor. The kid's legs tent out beneath her, then collect their length. William fits his hand into the loose rope coil and fashions a lead.

"She could eat you clean," Career says.

"I'll only keep her," William says, "if I can't find her right home."

The kid bucks up and stands on her hind legs like a circus trick, hopping twice before she clatters down. She resists the rope at her neck. "You want a tour, then?" William asks her, taking her on a short leash through the long, thin room of the Quinns' first floor. "It used to be more here," William explains, as if a goat needs an apology for the sparseness of the Quinns' living. "It used to be more, and it was clean."

"It's not so bad," Career says, and he should know, coming from half the size of William's life—only his Ma and him since before he can remember. Career leans against the window where the candle is lit, studying the damage of his sleeve.

"Doing with what we have," William says, except with Ma not working now it'll be no time at all before they lose even more than the less they've got.

The kid won't walk a straight line. She stops to taste everything she sees—the leg of the table, the brim of a pot, the pair of slippers Ma wore with the shawl she bought third-hand, down on St. Mary's Street. She stops at the bottles of the Nathan Brothers Rye and eats the heads off the curled up, dead daisies. She eats the singed stalks, too, and the crusted leaves, her ears flapping wild and strange. William fits his hand between the two nubs from where the horns will grow, and the kid bleats, pulls at its lead. She feasts on every dead flower in the Nathan Brothers row.

"You've got yourself a feeder," Career says.

"Dogs would have made a meal of her."

"She wouldn't have consented," Career says, as if he knows it for certain, "to being made a meal of."

"What do you think of Daisy?" William asks.

"What for?"

"To call her by, for the time being."

"You naming your goat now?"

"Goat needs a name," William says. "Every goat does."

The candlelight catches the jut of Career's chin. He shrugs.

"William?" Ma is calling from up the darkening stairs—the best she's done since Francis died, and William startles.

"It's me," he says. "Me and Career."

"Thought you'd brought a pony home."

"No, Ma. Ain't got a pony."

44

Career raises his dark brow and smiles. William's the kindest of liars.

"Daisy," William whispers, "you be a good girl now." He transfers the rope to Career and takes the split coat from his best friend's arms. "You watch her," he tells his friend. "And don't make trouble." William digs into the satchel for a needle and thread. He lights a second candle with the flame of the first and heads in Ma's direction.

"Career's in need of your touch," he tells her, rounding the corner on the last stair, and presenting the ruin of the jacket.

"I can't," she says, buried down deep in her sheets.

"Have to, Ma. Tomorrow's Career's big day. He's planning a sit-down with Mr. Childs." William pushes through her bedroom door and crosses toward her. He plants the candle on the table, beside the Kunkel's and the spoon. He reaches in to shadowy sheets and cups Ma's head in his hands. He folds the pillow behind her, fits her upright.

"Mr. Childs?" Ma asks, weary. "Mr. Childs of the *Ledger*?"

"That's the one." William opens the sack jacket to its split seam and brings the candle in close, sitting with Ma now, on the edge of her bed, while she adjusts her vision and fiddles with her pale and skinny hands. She turns the jacket for herself. Gives it the expert seamstress eye. Leans back again, exhausted with the effort.

"What were you boys doing?" she asks, at last.

"It was nothing, Ma."

"You weren't making trouble?"

"No, ma'am."

Downstairs there's the sound of scuffle and bleat. Career covers it all with a song, a high, sweet, holy version of "Safe in the Arms of Jesus." Ma takes a long and serious evaluation of her son, then straightens herself against the pillow.

"Here," she says, reaching for the needle and thread. "Let me at it."

Eleven

William chooses the sturdiest chair and puts the night watch on Daisy, giving her as much leash as she proves herself responsible to and feeding her the back end of the hard rye, which she chomps down in no time.

"Savor, Daisy," William says. But she won't.

They do a run of the street outside, for Daisy's business. They walk a clatter up and down, only the stars and the moon in the sky—the window at Mrs. May's gone dark, and Molly in her upstairs room, hoarding her penny.

"You're to be trusted," William tells the kid, reaching his hand through the dark to Daisy's muzzle and getting tongued. Her pulse races. Her ears flutter wild. William leaves his hand on her head between the nubs, telling her it'll be fine, and they'll search for her mama tomorrow, and there's nothing to worry on at the Quinns, until finally Daisy tucks her chin and settles. William feels the stillness come in, the hum of machines beyond, the black glisten of Career gone home, hanging his one good coat by the hook near his bed. In the halfway place between dream and sleep, Francis opens the front door and saunters in, the sun at his back and a milk cart trotting by, a tabby in the gutter swatting at the blue steam of the sky.

"That you, Francis?" William asks, and Francis only smiles— unbuttons his coat and it's a pantry inside. Fresh eggs and Oregon salmon, hominy and chestnuts, a buckwheat partridge that Ma will roast with the most everlasting care. Francis's legs are loose. His hands are white as a sea-bass belly.

"That you?" William asks. He strains against the dark, works hard to see. But it's only the song of restless engines thrumming against the hollow of William's hunger deep inside.

Twelve

In the morning the light is pink, pale, and rising. William suffers the stiff weave of the caning against the muscles of his back and a crick in his neck. There's a streak of tender burn across one palm and the tang of something sour at his feet, but William's eyes are two stones, and they won't focus — can't see the door through which Francis walked, his pockets heavy with brown eggs and sweets and the bright day vigilant around him.

"Were you going to tell me?"

William startles, tries to rouse himself out of the half place of the night. His hunger wakens and the room spins. The tang at his feet grows sharper.

"Ma?" He says it, won't believe it.

She takes a long, bleached breath. Draws the loose curls away from the bones of her face and leans in. Another figment playing visitation games, William thinks, and he's suddenly afraid that Ma's gone, too, that she's joined Francis in the after world, leaving William with no one but Pa, who's gone, too.

"There's a goat," the voice says, "at our table."

"Ma?" William asks again. He rubs his eyes open and sits up straight in the chair. He feels the tug of the rope against the burn on his palm and realizes that Daisy is braying. The kid's tasting the hem of Ma's skirt—Ma sitting catercorner at the table, her elbows brushing William's.

"I thought I heard a horse," Ma says.

"Just a goat, Ma," William manages.

"Just a goat and a goat's morning messes." Ma nods toward the floor and William understands at last what has sent the tang up from the planks beneath the table—understands that Ma's not dead, that she's come downstairs on her own.

"Daisy," William says, and Ma says, "Goat's got a name?"

"Yes, ma'am."

"You were planning on telling me?"

William scratches the rising itch along his neck. It's Ma, all right, in her violet nightdress, those slippers, the color of marigolds, on her feet. The blue throb of a vein runs crooked down her forehead. The place where her nose broke once collects the shine of the coming sun. "What are you doing up, Ma?" William asks.

"What are we doing with a goat?"

"She's a rescue," William says, and then, "The rye's gone, Ma, but there's tea."

Thirteen

The third time William hurries back home with a handful of bush twig, Ma's not downstairs, the goat either. All the heat of the day inside, but none of Daisy's fussing.

"Ma?" William calls, throwing his hat to the table and taking the stairs up, two at a time, the tips of the leafy sticks scratching the stairwell stucco. The upstairs heat hits him like the bottom of a pan.

"Daisy?"

He turns the corner into Ma's room, where the heat haze rises from the faded floor and William sees, out of the corner of one eye, the dove on the sill, its small heart high in its breast and its wings opening and settling, its eyes turned toward the bed where William sees the kid curled up in the spot beside Ma, its chin nestled into its tucked hooves. Ma's face is flushed, her loose curls beading. Daisy's coat is damp with sweat. The fringe of her ears brushes Pa's pillow.

"You're a good goat, then," William says, as now he lays the stolen branches onto the floor and fits himself across the foot of the bed. He catches his breath, lets the worrying ease.

A memory comes back, from years ago: Ma and Pa in their proper places and William and Francis, so much smaller back then, curled just like this at the base of their bed, listening to Ma tell her stories. She was fervent for the Union. She knew the names of the troops coming through and the places they'd come from—New England, New York, New Jersey—and when the Union Volunteer Refreshment Saloon went up down on Washington and Swanson, Ma was there, with the other wives, the clerks, the stucco men, the doctors off their duty—all of them serving those pickles and pies, those potatoes and cakes, that ham and beef and poultry. The soldiers came by way of train, direct from the ports of the Delaware and down Washington Avenue, and you knew they were coming, Ma said, by the cannon that went off and the rush of the brass band to take its place along the rails and the general happy will of the volunteers whose job it was to respite the soldiers from the bloody battlegrounds.

"We were an uncountable crowd," Ma would say, proud, Pa's arm around her as she talked, Francis and William at the base of the bed, neither of them ever interrupting. "We were ready."

Those long tables beneath the refreshment tent and the barrels of coffee and the quiet places, too, where the soldiers would take their rest or write their letters, which would be mailed to their proper homes for free. Sometimes Ma and the ladies would take to repairing the burst seams in the soldier's frock coats, or to patching the worn-down trouser threads, or to finding a replacement button. Sometimes they'd visit the ones gone direct to medical care—taking dictation for letters home, or giving them a hand to hold until the mercy of sleep took them in. Sometimes they'd stand in attendance on the burial grounds, and those were the days that Ma would come home sad, honoring the men who had passed with a poem someone told. "They're just boys," she would say, and neither Francis nor William nor Pa would say a word. These were Ma's stories, and Ma's losses, her long journey, three days each week, from Spring Garden to Southwark, traveling by foot and by horse trolley, sometimes by train.

"You're going to wear yourself thin, Essie," is all Pa would say. But there was no stopping Ma, all alive with her purpose, and no reason to try, because Ma was happy standing there on the right side of the cause.

William listens to the sounds of Ma's sleep, the quick sharp breaths and then the silence. He wonders how she talked the kid up the stairs, or if Daisy herself had insisted. It doesn't matter, either way. The one looking after the other is how William figures it, and Ma's sleep a rhythm to which William finally yields.

Fourteen

William wakes to the hard knock of Career's fist against the Quinns' front door. Daisy has made her way to the foot of the bed, chewing at the branches William brought home. Ma has turned in her sleep toward the wall. William gathers the goat into his arms. "It's Career," he tells her. "You'll see."

Career's pipe is lit, his cap pulled low when William opens the door to greet him. He raises that brow of his and saunters in, a bundle of *Ledgers* under his arm.

"You have your set down?" William asks. "With Mr. Childs?"

"Almost," he says. "I will."

Career lifts his chin and pulls the smoke out of the bowl of his pipe, letting his grin widen over the gaps between his teeth. He's walked a long way to save the seven cent fare, and the smells of the day are in the seams of his jacket—horse manure and boiler heat, the acid stink of newsprint, the crack smell of split lumber and coal chips. In William's arms, Daisy squirms. He takes her outside on her rope for some quick business and returns to find Career at the table with his *Ledgers* split wide to the classifieds. Career has poured some pitcher water into one of Ma's old pans and set it by his feet, and Daisy settles in for a drink.

"She's a smart one," Career says, with a prideful nod.

"She's going places," William says, like he and the goat have discussed it.

"Found something," Career says. "Brought it to you for a look." He runs his index finger down the *Ledger* pages, his nails chewed short and crooked. William's eyes follow at their own speed, Mrs. Allerbach's voice in his ear from his third year of schooling over at Lincoln, the best year, when Pa was still a semiskilled at Baldwin's and hadn't gone loose yet on the Nathan Brothers' Rye. Mrs. Allerbach said there were no rewards in speed when it comes to reading, that the smartest understanding starts slow. Outside, in the streets, Molly's calling for a game of penny pitch, and at William's feet Daisy drinks, but William is concentrating, studying hard, taking his time with the classifieds.

"See what it is?" Career asks.

"What's that?"

"Last eight days of classifieds and nobody's put a search on for a white kid."

"I see it."

"You'll be safe then. To keep her."

"She'll be a handful."

"Goats usually are."

William reads the classifieds again—every single one a story. There's an old terrier dog, large tusks in its low jaw and blue curly hair on its neck, that hasn't been seen for a week; liberal reward for its finding. There's twenty dollars at stake for a setter dog of roan color, and equal rewards for

56

a pure white Persian, strong and cobby, that goes by the name of Gemma. A gray-spotted pig with a pink-coiled tail was last seen near Twenty-first and Locust, and for the finding of it, fifteen dollars will be paid.

"You see this?" William asks.

"Of course I seen it. I brought it."

"It's a fortune being offered, for finding."

"Always is. LOST pages the best pages of the *Ledger*."

"Looks like someone's got to do it."

Career leans in close from across the table and exhales little clouds of pipe smoke. He shakes his head and smiles. William waits for the smoke to clear, then studies the Classifieds again, start to finish, pushing Career's smoke out of the way when it comes in near and obstructing.

REWARD—Lost on Thursday evening, a small brown Terrier Dog. Please return to 1524 Christian street.

LOST—Last Month, an Orange and white Setter Dog, name of owner, Max Hellmich and name of dog, Spank, with former residence of owner on collar. $30 reward if returned to 2314 Callowhill street.

$20 REWARD—LOST—Black aged tan female, long ears, answers to the name of Fanny. A liberal reward if returned to 1207 Locust street.

LOST between the Drove Yard and the residence of the subscriber, a red heifer marked on the right rump with a white stroke. Payment made upon retrieval.

"You think I've got a talent for it?" William asks, thoughtful.

"For finding, you mean?" Career chomps on the end of his pipe, considers.

"For finding and for taking care?"

Career studies William then looks past him to the goat. He takes a long suck on his pipe, drawing his cheeks in thin, then fattening them back up. "Course you do," he says.

"These papers to spare?" William asks, and when Career nods yes, William studies them again—not just the ads now, but the stories. The things lost and the things found and the promises the doctors make. E.F. Kunkel. Mr. Van Dyke. Dr. Radway and his Sarsaparilla Resolvent. William folds the Classifieds one by one and fits them onto the shelf that holds Ma's cooking spoons, out of reach of Daisy. Out in the street, Molly's still yelling for a game of pitch and Mrs. May is calling back, telling Molly that she's too old for this, that it's time she go in and help her Mama with the baby.

"It's getting late," William says.

Career squints through the clouds of his pipe smoke to study the sky beyond the window. "There's time," he says. When he bends low to collect Daisy, she licks the corner of his face, beneath one ear; she chews at the hair that has fallen from his cap. "Guess you're a Quinn now," he tells her, and she talks right back. William leaves a note for Ma, should she get up and come down and wonder where they're gone to.

Fifteen

The dark will come in, but not yet. Right now there are only stars and an orange moon, its quarter face out there floating the river. Daisy's got the trick of the lead already and is out in front, the stray cats keeping their distance and Molly calling on, and one of Molly's brothers, William can't tell which, is saying, "Molly, you let the boy alone," but Molly's got a penny that she's aching to return. "You practice with it," Career calls out behind him, and Molly lets out a long, despairing cry, like she can't bear to keep what she's borrowed for a single second more. "Play you tomorrow," Career says, but Molly won't trust him this time.

"Girl thinks she's going to marry you," William says, when they're out of earshot.

"Girls are like that," Career says. William thinks of his parasol girls — the sameness of them, the strange business of their mother. He looks up, as if he can hope them into passing, but it's just Daisy, yammering forward.

They walk along and keep their silence. They watch the evening grow long and grow wide. They take the familiar road, piece their way across the train tracks, pass the train shed, wait for Daisy to eat whatever it is she finds, her chomping-in a sound of gratitude. William feeds his hunger with thoughts of Mrs. May's soup, which he'll collect tomorrow, adding another fifteen cents to the list of debts he's come to owe. "You pay me when you can," Mrs. May will tell him, and he'll feel his face burn like it always does for the slide the Quinns have come to.

Now William thinks of Francis keeping them in food. He thinks of the Quinn kitchen in the months after Pa got caught, the Grossner's sheets dripping dry, the work his Ma would do. They'd have fowl for dinner, not hominy. They'd have coffee proper with milk and sugar cubes, and at the end of it all, Francis would say he had a surprise, and out from some stealth neither Ma nor William ever saw, he'd slip a box and untie its string.

"Close your eyes, Ma," Francis would say, and Ma would, her face catching the gleam from the pails of bleach on the floor.

"What do you want more than anything, Ma?" Francis would ask.

"Pa," she'd say. "First of all, Pa." Her eyes trembled beneath their lids. Her hair curled an undefeated blonde.

"And after that?"

"Cornstarch pudding. Coconut pie. A slice of lemon sponge cake."

"You like a peach pie, Ma?"

"You know I do."

"You open the box, you see what's inside."

William never knew how his only brother did it—how he'd turn that first floor room with its bleach and wash for hire, its absence of Pa, the crackle of the Grossner sheets, into fresh fowl and sugar cubes and pie when pie was in season. Francis did, that's all William knew. Francis could.

"Eat your pie now," Francis would say, and Ma would—delicate pieces with delicate fingers, her pinky extended, ladylike. Later, in the room that the brothers shared, Francis would lie back, kick off his boots, and make like he had nearly forgotten the square of chocolate in his pocket.

"Had my fill," Francis would say. "This piece is yours."

"You sure about it, Francis?"

"I'm sure."

"You going to tell me how?" William would ask it, the chocolate melting on his tongue. He'd make it last. He'd wake and taste it later.

"Nothing to it."

But there was something to it that Francis never told. There was something, and it grew, and while Francis slept in the bed across from William, those secrets swelled like a fist.

"You think your Pa hears us coming?" Career asks William now, Daisy bobbing up ahead, weaving and tucking, having her say on whatever it is that her big eyes are seeing. No girls have passed, the machine sounds are lulling, and through the windows of Preston Retreat come the cries of a baby who won't be comforted, of a mother shushing and cooing, of the splash of water into a basin—ward life for the indigent married. The building is proud and sturdy as a bank—risen up and massive and crowned with a cupola, and Daisy is pulling sideways toward it, wanting to leap the low stone wall to get a taste of the garden beyond.

"I think Pa hears us when we come," William answers.

"You think he suspects on Daisy?"

61

"Don't see why not."

Daisy strains at her rope until William stoops to collect her. She bucks and knocks about in his arms, bleats like that baby overhead. William talking to her knows she can't be talked to; she has the smell of the Preston garden in her and won't leave without a sampling.

"All right, then," William says, and he leaps the low wall, Daisy up with him like a bundle. There's fir along the edge and spruce, tulip poplar, sugar maple, magnolia that is pink perfume in April, but Daisy's eager for the sweet bursts along the low interior hedge, and William slips in, quick, to snap three blue heads from a hydrangea. "Be quick," he tells Daisy, "and quiet," but she's only quick, not quiet. When she's done, William weaves through the trees and slips back out toward the street, thin as a shadow coming. Out on the walk, Career waits like an old man, sucking on the end of his pipe.

"You see that?" Career asks.

"See what?" William asks, breathless.

"Those lookalikes of yours," Career says. "Up in the Preston window."

William turns quick but sees nothing—not in any window, not on any of the floors. Just a fat old nurse in white, a baby bobbing in each of her arms, giving the boys a stern look from the second floor.

"I don't see any girls."

"They were there," Career says. "I swear on it."

William scans the windows again, the verandah, the wide portico. He waits, but the dark is coming.

"You want to see your Pa, we better start walking," Career advises.

"I know it."

"They'll be back."

William shrugs. "It doesn't matter." He releases Daisy and she pulls ahead, and William thinks of Pa, in his cell on the Hill, the night sky coming in through the circle above and the guardsman down the corridor, watching. They've put Pa to work, according to the letters the Prison Society has sent home. Fitted out his cell for the caning work he has learned to master, and he canes, in solitude, taking his outside air thirty minutes of every day in the exercise pen that is connected to his room. There are newspapers up at Cherry Hill, but Pa couldn't read them. There's a library with six thousand books, and someone willing to help Pa learn, but Pa prefers the work, according to the letters the Society writes for him—the handwriting so neat, the words proper. William is the one who has written back—representing, Francis would say, for the Quinns. He's the one who's told Pa the things that he thinks Pa would like to hear—true things he's embroidered on—telling him nothing about Francis. A man can't live with the dying of his son, and William knows Pa won't survive if he knows he's lost his Francis. *You listen for our whistle, Pa.* That's what William's written. *We come just ahead of the black part of night.*

"What do you think Pa thinks on," William asks Career, spotting a kicking stone on the street ahead but letting it be, for Daisy seems asleep in his arms and he knows better than to disturb her.

"Time," Career says. "Probably."

"A mind full of regrets," William says.

"It wasn't his fault, what happened," Career says.

"Not at first," William says. "Anyway."

His name was Frank Doyle, and he lived down on Hamilton, at the corner of Thirteenth. Had a kid he called Knickers, though his born name was Matty. Doyle was ambitious for that odd boy's sake—taking on extra shifts and doing any work he could talk his way through. What happened happened near Christmas, and Knickers, Doyle had been overheard to say, was due for a new suit, a pair of new boots, too, and any work that was needed extra, Doyle would gladly do. He'd come early and he'd stay. He'd ask around. He'd offer.

Pa had a dozen years at the Works on him by then—earning his pay through the piecework and getting along in the Baldwin smith shops, the machine shops, the back yard of the Crystal Palace; they called Pa Easy, and he was. At home Pa talked trains—the five thousand separate parts that wardrobe out a locomotive, the flexible beams and variable motions that ride them smooth, the smokestack feedwater heater that no one but the engineers understood, the latest instigations for the refining driver brakes.

Pa called the trains by their names—Old Ironsides, Ten Wheeler, the 4-4-0—and Ma always said, as he sat at supper talking, "You'll be manager someday."

The worst day of Pa's life up until the matter with Doyle was the day Matthias Baldwin, head of the whole Works, died, and the blackest William thought Pa would ever be was on the day of the great man's funeral, when the whole city, it seemed, and near about every Baldwin worker, marched the circuit around the Works as the Baldwin cupola bell tolled. "We were a thousand," Pa would say, as if one thousand were a destitute showing for one of the nation's finest men. Two weeks later Pa took an orchid up to Laurel Hill and placed it on the Baldwin grave. Spent a week's worth of wages for the privilege.

Pa and Doyle were friends when the accident went down. They were pieceworkers of a certain kind—known for working hard and staying on, and so when the call came for a few good men down at the new building at Broad and Buttonwood, Pa and Doyle were among the counted. It was a Monday, December 14, 1868. It was cold as it should be outside, the frosted air on the windows like snow flattened and held, and the job was a hoisting job—quick, they said, and easy. Doyle offered to come in with the others on a guy-rope end, even though, as it was later proven in the court of law, Doyle had never worked a guy rope before, had never hoisted a rafter, didn't know the mechanics of derricks. Doyle had stepped in where he shouldn't have, thinking of boots for his son, and the other riggers, who knew nothing of Doyle and guy ropes either, didn't stop him, didn't teach him the trick about ropes and pins. The others were at fault, the jury said, for letting the bad thing happen. Pa was part of the others.

"I shouldn't have let him," Pa said after. "I shouldn't have." Over and over. Every drink Pa took since Christmas of '68 poured directly from what Pa should have done and failed to stop. It happened fast. It happened, but William could never understand it—how the rafter was hoisted into its proper place, and how Pa and Doyle and the other men began to move the derrick, as was hoisting protocol. The calamity began when the derrick tipped and fell and when the rope pulled taut and when the men working the rope were snapped sky high—reeled at once to the ceiling line, and left up there to dangle.

Pa was calling out to Doyle, "Help is coming. You can stand it now." Pa was calling and the men were holding on, but Doyle—he got the fear inside. He grew yellow, Pa said, in the skin, and bulged up around the eyes, and Pa was saying, "You do it, now, it can be done," but there was all that terror in Frank Doyle's eyes. "He let it go," Pa said. "Opened his fists and fell." And when Doyle fell, the rafter fell, too—came down hard and fast and struck the lame man on the head. Pa and the others caught up on the ropes had to wait until someone could reel them down—hung up there helpless, on the ceiling line, while Doyle lay below, his fall and the rafter falling making a half orphan of his son.

"Doyle knew nothing about rope slack, that's what the trouble was." Pa said it, but Pa blamed himself, didn't need a court to tell him what was done, how the damages were arranged—that kid Knickers losing his Christmas suit and boots and his father all in one. After the jurors ruled and put their censure on, after Pa was relieved of his piecework at the Works, Pa was nothing but long days and liquor—nothing Francis or Ma or William could have done.

"It's not mine anymore," Pa would say, and it wasn't just the 2-8-0s and the 4-6-0s and the 2-6-0s he was speaking of. It was the peaceable bargain that he'd made with his soul. Christmas of '68 and on, drink was Pa's single compromise.

Afterwards is when Ma started taking in the sewing and the laundry. It's when Francis got into the habit of bringing home things he couldn't explain the origins of, and when William stopped going to Lincoln. Sometimes William read to Mrs. May next door and she rewarded him with a coin, and sometimes he cleaned down at the Institute for the Blind on Race, but mostly William looked after Pa, Ma saying, "He just needs you by, William. Doesn't matter if he don't talk to you some."

"It's not your fault, Pa," William would say. But it was like Pa couldn't hear right anymore, and in the nights, when Pa opened the front door and closed it behind him, he begged William not to follow.

"Where you going, Pa?"

"Pa?"

In the mornings Pa would be back, red-eyed, the look of shame about him.

Now Career is busy with his tune and Daisy has agreed to be carried and the walking is easy in the cooling hour. Career has whistled sometimes and sucked at his pipe between songs, and they're cornering in on the unforgiving walls of the penitentiary. William feels the shadows grow longer. He senses the enormity of the penitentiary's silence.

"I went but he didn't show," William tells Career, and it doesn't take Career but a minute to understand who William is speaking of.

"The officer?"

"Socrates Kernon. The only one."

"You saying you took Daisy over to Norris House?"

"Daisy wasn't mine yet," William says. "This was two nights ago."

Career nods, gets it straight in his head. "You ask directly for him?"

"Nah. I sat there, waited."

"You have a plan?"

"I want to see him first, before I finalize my thinking."

Career produces a long, low whistle, gives William an appraising look. "Officer Socrates Kernon is a murderer," he says. "You need a plan."

"A murderer and a thief," William says. "Stealing from my brother."

"It can't be proven."

"I want what he took from us back."

"Francis isn't coming back," Career says, after a moment.

"It's true."

"And Kernon's with the law."

"I want what he stole."

"All right," Career says. "Then it'll be so."

"I hate him with all I have," William says.

"Of course you do. But you ain't seem him, yet?"

"Ain't see him, but I seen the lookalikes' mother."

"At Norris? Two nights ago?"

"Strangest thing," William says, and then explains how the woman came in, her face and posture stern, and went about her business with that parcel of magazines.

"She notice you?"

"I don't know."

"*Anyone* notice you?"

"The blowzy did. Made sure I had my supper."

Career turns and gives William a funny look. He knits his brows and says nothing else, because they've turned the corner onto Coates, and Daisy's waking up. William strokes her head and sets her down, lets her scramble to her senses. She yanks at her lead, but William holds firm. She pulls her ears back when Career starts to whistle.

"Make it a nice one now," William says, though he doesn't have to. Career gives his song everything he has, and William hopes it toward Pa's hearing. Daisy looks like she understands the tune, like she'd help if she could, like she wants to. The sound of wings overhead floats by, that dove again, always near.

"Night, Pa," William says, when Career's song is through.

"Top of the evening, Mr. Quinn."

Sixteen

Ma's asleep by the time William gets home. Daisy's done in by the walking. William fits the kid down on Pa's pillow and warns her to take care of things, to keep Ma safe for the time being. "You're in charge of things," he says, and the goat settles in. Ma reaches a hand out of her sleep and asks, "Francis?"

"Shhh, Ma," William says, leaning in, kissing her cheek. "I'm taking care of things."

"I was dreaming Francis," she says, opening her eyes in the dark.

"You get your sleep, Ma," William tells her. "Daisy's here. She's had a long walk. She's peaceful."

"Francis would have laughed at you," Ma says, murmurs it, like she's still mostly sleeping. "Petting up with a goat."

"I wouldn't have let him."

"He'd have been bringing her home some of that pie."

"I miss Francis's pie."

"I miss Francis," Ma says. "All the time." She takes a long breath in, and when she exhales she shivers. Daisy talks and Ma lies there listening. The room grows finally quiet.

I'd like to fix things, Ma, William doesn't say. *I'd like to get back what the cop stole, get it for your sake, Ma. I plan on it. I promise.*

Doesn't say it because he can't promise, because promising the particulars is lying. "I'll be back, Ma," is what he says instead, when he knows that she is sleeping. He fits his hand between Daisy's ears, strokes the warm hard soft spot between her horn buds. "You keep her safe, Daisy," he says, laying out the terms of a make-do promise, "and tomorrow I'll take you back to Preston."

Seventeen

Maybe, William thinks, Pearl lives right here, at the bar. She's turned the cuffs of her lavender sleeves to her elbows, let loose the wild springs of her hair, allowed the tangerine hem of her overskirt to collect the splinters of the tavern's thick-planked floor. A necklace of sweat presses against her collar. The ruches, flounces, frills, and pleats of her underskirt fall freely.

"Why, look who it is," she says, now that he's pushed through the door—stands there in the gusting kitchen smoke, eyes adjusting to the sheen and kerosene, to Pearl, wearing the same dress as before.

Old Murphy stares up from where he's been ragging down the bar, tucks one finger behind an ear, and scratches hard, like he's thinking. "It was oysters, wasn't it, boy? Oysters and beer?"

"Mister?" William asks, walking into the blue bands of smoke and studying the shadows in the room, the corners: no Kernon.

Pearl sits straighter on her stool. Bryant, beside her, wakes from a snore. The man with the sausage face is gone. The man with the newspaper tent is gone, too, his pile of news in a heap where he left it. Scattered all along the bar are used bottles and discarded plates, that magazine where the woman left it. Norris House is empty but for Pearl and Bryant, for Old Murphy at the bar and Jerry in his kitchen, the smell of eggs and oysters, hot pepper.

"You're looking lost, kid," Pearl announces to William.

"I ain't lost, ma'am." Because William's right where he means to be, making good on his promise to Ma.

"It's oysters you want?" Old Murphy repeats himself.

William digs into his pocket, pulls out five cents, courtesy of a coin he found this morning in Francis's sock. "I can pay," William says, "if you're wondering."

Pearl tosses her head back and laughs, shows the holes in her mouth where teeth are missing. She fans her face with her hand, hurries along a cloud of smoke. When she speaks again she's wheezing. "Ain't he a dignified one," she says to Bryant.

"Indeed he is."

"Not here for the charity."

Bryant rubs his nose. "A boy raised proper."

William feels his face go hot as the pots in Jerry's kitchen. "I'm looking for someone," he explains.

"Are you now?"

"The officer," William says it fast, name like a burn on his tongue. "Officer Kernon."

Pearl looks from William to Bryant to Old Murphy and back. She fans her hand again, the smoke somehow assisting with her thinking. "You in some sort of trouble?" she asks after a while.

"I am not."

"What do you need an officer for?"

74

"He has something that belongs to me."

"Officer Kernon?"

"I want it back."

"You calling the officer a thief, boy?"

"William," he says. "That's my name. William. You can call Kernon what you want."

Bryant blows a long, low whistle through his two spacious front teeth, rubs at the bald place on his head, leaving it to shine beneath the flickering kerosene. Old Murphy shakes his head and turns away, not wanting full knowledge of the fussing.

"You know what you're asking for?" Pearl asks, after a while. She pulls her hair into her hands and lets it go—big wild puff.

"Yes, ma'am."

"Officer Kernon is a cop. A *mean* cop."

William swallows over the rising lump in his throat. "I know that's true."

"I wouldn't be messing with a cop, William," Pearl says. She has a faraway smell to her, like old perfume. When she lifts her arms, the smell comes closer.

"It's family business," William says, suddenly stubborn, because stubborn is part of courage, isn't it? He'd like to ask Francis.

"Family, that's it?" Pearl crosses her arms beneath the whale of her chest and studies William with squinting eyes until finally William understands that he'll have to confess if he wants anybody's help catching Kernon.

"He stole from the Quinns."

Bryant whistles again. Pearl touches the collar of stains at her neck. Jerry comes from the kitchen with a plate in his hand. Two oysters. One egg. Plenty of pepper. He slaps it down for Pearl but she slides it one place over and gives Bryant an elbow in the ribs. "Make room," she tells him, and then to William, "You tell us all about it." She rubs at the stool where Bryant's been sitting, polishes it smart, waves her big hands in William's direction. In the heat, in the smoke, William stands.

"Kernon's a rat," Pearl says. "We know he is. You eat your eggs first. Take your time before you say it."

"I didn't order eggs with the oysters, ma'am," William says, the steam of it rising to him and tempting the hollow that lives beneath his ribs.

"Eggs is on Bryant, oysters is, too," Pearl says, and Bryant makes a long, low whistle until Pearl reaches across, gives him a quick slap on the face.

"Now what was that for?" Bryant asks, rubbing the hot spot.

"You keep your manners," she says to him, and then to William, "You start where it begins."

William sits, reluctant and famished. Old Murphy finds a fork, holds it near. "It's a long story, ma'am," William says.

"We don't mind."

"Starting with my father before getting to my brother, and plenty of mean in between." He says it and then he wonders why he said so much. Wonders if these people can be trusted—this prostitute, her sometimes man, the men who water them up, put their eggs beside their oysters.

"We'll get to what we get to."

"It's my Ma I'm worried on."

"Course it is. Ma is important."

Pearl's nose, William thinks, might have been delicate. Her eyes, catching the light, have a little beauty. She's right there beside him, her chin in one hand, Bryant to the left of her, twirling a cord of her hair with his hand. Old Murphy pours out five beers and hands one each to each, and Jerry leans his across the bar, wiping his face with his apron.

"Eggs look good with the oysters," William says at last. Because it's like the eggs are still cooking, right there on the plate, the lacey sizzle on the edges growing sweeter. William cradles the fork in his hand until his hand decides for him. Breaks the bubble of one egg, and the plate swims yellow, and William thinks about Pa and about Francis. *Man of the house.*

"Story's about honor, ma'am," William says, and it's a good egg, well-made. It goes just right with the oyster, the generous spray of pepper. Somewhere outside a horse is impatient, and the moon is rising, and the trains are sleeping shiny in their sheds. Ma's upstairs in her bed and Daisy's keeping watch. William has come to keep his promise.

"I knew it would be, judging from your character."

"You can't know my character, ma'am."

"I can," she says. "I do."

"You know Officer Kernon?" William asks.

She nods.

"He took from you?"

"He's a bad man," she says. "It's proven."

"You think you can help me?"

"Depending on what you need," she says. "Depending on the shape of your story."

Eighteen

It's three hours more before William pushes back out the Norris House door and into the black of the night—two fresh eggs in his pocket, thanks to Pearl's insisting: *You take them home to your Ma.* Moon glisten rides the rails up Pennsylvania Avenue. From the bell tower above the Works, that mourning dove looks eerily down, collecting her wings to her chest.

"I'm looking out for you, Francis," William says, so that only the bird can hear, and maybe also that horse that's passing in a hitch ahead of the hackney cab. "I'm doing you proud." The loose stones in the rail bed click beneath William's boots, but it's the sound of Pearl Bright that William still hears, her words hovering near: *You let us use the logic on Kernon. Revenge would cost you dear.*

The moon's a sickle. The stars outshine the Bush Hill soot, the long, thick skin of the manufactories, the spike of pipes and refuse yards. Up above, the dove takes off and flies northwest toward the prison. "You see that?" William asks Francis. "You see her coming for Pa?" But the only answer is the skip of the rocks, the hesitation of the horse halfway across the width of Broad.

William doesn't hear the plaintive mewling until he reaches Eighteenth, and when the sound makes its way to him, he wonders if a baby has somehow escaped from Preston Retreat—a stupid idea and one that soon corrects itself as William's sees, down the way, a heifer caught up in the tracks, its tail whacking frantic at its own buttocks.

Eggs in his pocket, pepper on his tongue, William runs quiet as he can, his feet on the ties and not the ballast. The closer he gets, the clearer he sees how the heifer's tail beats and her ears flatten and her three hooves stomp in protest of the fourth, which has dug itself into some trouble.

"You'll be fine," William says, as he comes nearer. "Now let me at you, I ain't a hurter." The heifer's weight crunches the ballast and her tail swats around like a rope and under the moon, her red coat shivers and folds. "We're just talking, now," William says, his voice calm. "We're just having us a conversation, you and me." The heifer stares back mournful and afraid with her big, soft, fringed eyes—moaning and mewling and mooing. Above the caught hoof the flesh is sliced and worrisome, the terror in the heifer's eyes most worrisome of all.

"What are you doing out here?" William asks, so he can distract her. "What did you say your name was?" Talking like that and inching closer by the moment, easing in, stepwise fashion, toward the heifer's panic, until now, close enough, William sees the white stroke on the right rump and remembers the words in the *Ledger*. *Lost between the Drove Yard and the residence of the subscriber. . .*

"You're a long way from home, aren't you now?" William says, crouching to his knees and putting his hand out to the heifer's hot breath. She

81

shudders and brawls and then of a sudden lowers her head, relinquishing her defense, as if this were both her prayer and her confessing.

"You think you'll let me see that?" William asks, putting his one hand out toward the stuck hoof and touching not the hurt place but the shank above—a careful, gentle petting, more words for more distracting. "I got me a goat named Daisy," William's saying, his voice low and calm. "You believe that? A goat of my own. Left her taking care of my Ma." The heifer not saying one way or the other, but soon leaving William to the business of stroking and at the same time levering the railroad tie away from the ballast, a freeing operation. When the foot breaks loose, the heifer yelps. She circles lame, but can't go far.

"You're going to heal up," William says, easing out of the crouch and watching the heifer in her hurt dance. "I promise you will." But the heifer is dazed by her freedom and hurt, and William understands that there's no choice for it; he slips the belt from around his waist and comes in close to loop it firm around the animal's neck.

"We'll get you home," William says. "Break of day, we'll get you to it." But for now they're headed to Carleton Street, where Ma, William hopes, is fast asleep under Daisy's guard.

"I'm going to tell you a story," William tells the heifer. And then he tells it like he told it to Pearl, keeping the animal keen on him and not on its own hurt in the slow limp home.

Nineteen

Ma had only just lit the low wick on the candle and put the barley soup over the fireplace flame when the knock came at the door, the terrible shouting. There were four bowls out on the table, four spoons, and the third time that the voice outside hollered "*Quinn!*" William himself went to the door and jimmied the latch, and this is the moment he can't forgive in himself—the moment that stopped him short in the telling to Pearl and the moment that stops him here, heading south, talking a lost heifer half its way home. William jimmied the latch and let the law push through. William stood there and it was done, and soon as William turned and saw the bottom of Pa's worn-down boots flying up the narrow stairs, saw the man with the uniform swearing and running, he knew that whatever he'd allowed would not be fixed.

"Don't," Ma was saying. "Don't, don't, don't." But the stranger was quick up the stairs—the law with its jacket and stick. "Martin Quinn, you cannot beat the law! Martin Quinn, you have been found!"

Francis was hurtling up the steps behind the law and Pa both, grabbing at the first with the skinny of his arms, grabbing and being kicked back, dirt on his face, a bruise, and all the while, Ma was weeping, "Don't," into the kettle of soup, the old ladle. "Don't," she kept saying, until William was scrambling up the stairs too, his feet slipping beneath him, his eyes fixed on Francis, who was fixed on the law, who was chasing Pa, the sound of Pa's boots overhead. From upstairs William heard the boots on the landing, and he heard them in the hall, and then he heard them running the channel between his own bed and Francis's, toward the room's one window, two stories up from the street.

"Don't!" Ma cried, but they could hear the sound of the sash being torn from the sill, the jolt of Pa's flight through the air. They heard the snap of a thigh bone, and Pa's poor, hoarse cry. Ma dropped the kettle and flew—through the front door, wide open as the law had left it. Pa in the street saying, "My love, forgive me." Pa's head in Ma's aproned lap, and his leg scribbled out in the wrong direction, William and Francis at the window looking helplessly down.

They wouldn't hear about Pa for days. They wouldn't know what was being done and how he was accused and where they took him, until somebody said, by way of Mrs. May, "Your poor old Pa won't be the same." Nobody goes into Cherry Hill and comes out their own version of sane. It's a cage and the sky is watching. The mind turns to the life it has lost.

"He wasn't a forger," Ma'd say. "Not your Pa. He couldn't have."

"He's still Pa," Francis would say back. "Still our Pa. We know it, Ma."

But it was after Pa's arrest that Francis began to stay out all night and come home smelling like the innards of a barn. For a while that was the point:

Francis came home. Afternoons, he'd talk himself into some poor version of a job—delivering, running, stocking—then forfeit the post for whatever reason he could find, making the whole thing out to be an escapade for Ma. "The boss was a drunk," he'd explain over supper later. "Facts is the facts, Ma. He was. Sent me down to the docks with bad instructions and when I came back he was fast asleep, a fly on the ridge of his nose. I liked the hat, Ma, look. A souvenir. We'll take it down to St. Mary's tomorrow and barter you a nightgown."

Days went on like this, weeks, but somehow Francis provided—fresh eggs in the inside pockets of his coat, a can of fish, a pound of butter, a hank of venison that Ma would roast in the evening with the most everlasting care, as if it were the first meal, or the last, or a gift she'd tunnel through to Pa in the silent penitentiary. She dreamed, she said, of digging a tunnel through to Pa, of whispering a warm word in. Francis made friends with the hominy man, the chestnuts man, the tripe seller, and one early afternoon, Francis came home with a live rabbit in a pink hatbox—a fuzzy thing that he'd found along the Schuylkill in a patch of wild corn. "Quinn's got a rabbit. In the hatbox. Hear it? Quinn has got his supper."

The more Francis was gone, the more he knew to stay away—missing suppers, missing sleep, not rolling down Carleton or up the stoop until around noon the next day, keeping a fist around his secrets, a big fist. "Where've you been?" William would demand of Francis, after he'd sneak in through their bedroom door, smelling like the docks, or the market. Smelling like gin.

"Nothing to report," Francis would say, murmur it or smear it, a smile breaking across his face, like one of those plank bridges, William thought, that somebody flung across the Wissahickon.

"Pa's already in jail," William would say. "Quinns can't afford another."

"Someone has to provide," Francis would say.

"Ma don't want it this way."

"Ma don't have to know, does she?" Francis would ask, sitting on the side of his bed waiting for William to respond.

But William didn't know what justice was, and Ma wasn't home—was out with a basket beneath one arm, delivering a bundle of clean sheets, picking up bleach, collecting the linens and the sewing for tomorrow's load. Francis would lie back, skinny, on his bed, then sit up straight, hoisting one arm over the bony ridge of his shoulders and digging at an itch on his back. He'd close his eyes to yawn, then keep them closed like that and sit there, half tilted, as if chasing some kind of windmill dream. And then, his knees sometimes skimming up against William's, Francis would start to talk about all the things he wanted, all the promises he was storing up for Ma. A Wallace & Blackiston carriage and a pair of horses to pull it far. E. Burthey Cream Drops, French Vanilla, from 324 South Third. A pantry full of spiced Schlect & Jamieson fish. A clutch of orchids from Bisele's on Eleventh.

And then January, last year, Francis came home lit up and nervous with a rumor he had heard. "They're calling it the Phasmatrope," he said. "They say it makes pictures move."

"Pictures don't move," William told him, sure, at least, of that.

"They will," Francis said. "I heard them talking at the market. Phasmatrope is coming, and you and me is taking Ma."

"Where's it coming to?" William asked, looking slantwise at Francis, suspending his trust.

"To the Academy."

"*Moving* pictures at the Academy," William repeated.

"Waltzing figures," Francis said. "And acrobats. Think of it, William. Think of Ma."

But William was thinking of the moving pictures, better than a Zoetrope, Francis said. He was thinking of stepping into the Academy itself—the chandelier and its glitter lights, the moneyed people in their boxes. "We could never afford it," William said.

"We could." Francis was absolute. "We are."

"We're out of eggs, is what we are," William said. "And the water rent is coming due. Regular rent, too."

"Will you listen to yourself?"

"What?"

"An old man already."

"Somebody's got to take care of things, Francis. Somebody has to be watchful."

"I'm taking care of the things that matter, William."

"Tell that to Ma."

"Ma will love the Phasmatrope."

"Ma won't love you getting into trouble, Francis, which is the only way the Quinns would ever ticket up at the Academy."

"Swear, William."

"Swear what?"

"Swear you won't tell Ma."

"Why shouldn't I?"

"Because it's a surprise, that's why."

Outside there was snow, wet and gray. Downstairs the fire had gone untended and the cold had begun to seep through, and Francis, despite his being out and wild all night, could not stop himself from smiling.

"You've already done it, haven't you?" William asked then.

"Done what?"

"Gone and got the tickets for Ma."

"Got the tickets for the three of us, is what I've done."

"How, Francis?"

"How does it matter?" Francis flopped down across his bed, brought his knees to his chin, and closed his eyes, as if the magnitude of his achievement had done him in. An old fly had taken refuge in their room.

"It's the water rent that's due," William said, after a while. But Francis said nothing; Francis couldn't. He was fast asleep and snoring in his bed. William sat watching that fly circle his head. A family of forgers, he thought. A family of thieves.

Twenty

The sickle moon is low and the sun is rising. Across the way, at Thomas Wood, the machines that make the machines are waking to the business of spooling, winding, beaming, dyeing, sizing, scouring, shafting. In that funny place between dream and knowing, William hears the heifer behind him—her voice like an engine, her belly a warm, soft spot for William's head.

"What are you making a spectacle of yourself for?"

It's Molly, little Molly, standing above him, her fists punched to her hips, her hair already falling out of its sloppy yellow bow. She's wearing one brother's shirt and another's pants. Her feet are bare and dirty.

"You can't bring a heifer into a house, now can you, Molly?" William asks, his tongue still sticky with the agitated taste of oysters, eggs, and beer.

"But what you got a heifer for in the first place?" She rubs one eye as if she's just waking, too. As if she's somehow stumbled onto the wrong Carleton Street, at the wrong time of day, the wrong decade.

"Found her," William says. He sits up straight against the heifer's back, and she moos again, her engines churning. She slaps at the street with the rope of her tail and chews at her cud, moist and noisy. William tries to remember how long he's been out here, pillowed up with the heifer, both of them dead tired from all the talking and the traveling.

"She yours now?"

"She is not."

"You going to keep her anyway?"

"Now why would I do that?"

"Why would you sleep on the street with a cow?" Molly asks, and just like that she plops down beside William and fits her head on a warm, red place. The heifer shudders and slaps her tail. Molly doesn't mind her.

"You be careful now."

"I'm always careful."

"I guess so," William says. "I guess you are." They lie there like that, side by side, against the heifer, letting the moon fall and the sun rise, the noise of machines up around them. Molly twitches her naked toes and yanks at her bow, and suddenly William's remembering the day of the cotton mill fire down on Twenty-fourth and Hamilton—how Molly ran back and forth, reporting on the progress of the fighters. Every time she'd come back, her face would be blacker, until finally even her mother came out and marched her inside for a scrub. Molly Harberger's a tenacious one. Someday, William thinks, she'll get her Career.

"Your friend going to keep his promise to penny pitch me?" she asks, like she can read the thoughts in William's head.

"I suppose he will."

"What's he acting so important for?"

"Because he is," William says. "Don't you know it?"

Molly shrugs and sucks at her thumb. The heifer moos, and she turns to pet it. "Keep your thoughts to yourself now," she tells it. "It's too early for most people's rising." The heifer lets out one long last exclaiming, then settles back down, its chin on the shin where the wound has already started healing.

"Your Ma ever going to lose her sadness?" Molly asks.

"She's had a hard spell."

"She ever going to teach me her sewing like she said she would?"

"I don't know."

"I wish that Francis didn't die," she says, crossing her arms to watch the rest of morning rise.

"I wish it, too." William remembers again the waltzing figures of the Phasmatrope, the somersaulting acrobat stopped clear and high and long, the delicate jewels of the Academy lights in Ma's green and tender eyes. Ma was young and she was brilliant on her Academy night, and whatever Francis had done for those tickets, whatever sleight of hand, small deceit, false promise, it had, William knew, been another version of right, another way of defending the soul. Francis's wrongs came from Francis's good; he was an innocent, slaughtered.

You let us use the logic on Kernon, Pearl Bright had said, end of the evening, a kiss on William's cheek when they were done. *Revenge would cost you dear.* But what was the logic, and where was Kernon, and what would Pa do, if he knew?

Twenty-one

"You walked her all the way to the Delaware?" Career's asking.

"I did."

"And she didn't complain?"

"Not much for a cow."

"And it was just like the *Ledger* promised?"

"Handsome reward, and the subscriber paid."

Career throws his head back and blows out a whistle, long and sweet. He cradles the bowl of his pipe in the palm of one hand, a Burthey cream drop in the other. "We have to share them, William," Ma had said, when she understood what William had done. A box wrapped up with a lavender bow. The kid goat to help untie it. The candy presented after they'd finished the tarts he'd bought at the bakery on Walnut.

"We'll go to the market, Ma," he'd told her. "Tomorrow. The two of us."

"Are we rich now, William?" she asked him, warily.

"For the time being," he said, "we are."

"You tell me how."

"Lost and rescue," he said.

"Lost and rescue, how?" she asked.

"It's gentleness, Ma. It's speed."

"Tell it again," Career is saying.

"Tell what?"

"How it is to be a wealthy one."

"You should know it."

"I'm not rich."

"How about the One Thing, Career. How about the secret you won't tell?"

"That's for the future," Career says. "That isn't now. What does the wealth feel like right now?"

"Like the luck was on me," William finally says.

"To luck, then," Career says, raising his pipe and clinking a patch of low sky.

The fireflies with their lanterns have started to arrive. Daisy tugs toward Preston Retreat. Beneath the umbrella of an old tulip tree, along the low stone wall, she stops. William scoops her into his arms and climbs into the shade of the garden, telling Daisy to keep her voice low, loosening the lead. In a room upstairs, someone sings a lullaby.

"Hurry on, Daisy," William tells the kid, and the nurses in the windows come and go and the mothers sing and the babies cry. Daisy tugs at her lead and William lets her free among the heads of sweet hydrangea.

"That's enough, now," William says. "You don't be greedy." Shortening the lead, reeling her in, hearing the clacking of heels through the front vestibule, across the porch, between the giant Grecian columns. Through the covert green of the bushes and trees, William sees the lookalikes' mother hurrying out and down, and after her, some distance behind, the girls themselves, their buttoned boots shushing in their mother's wake. A dark horse and hansom cab wait along Hamilton Street. The mother turns, impatient.

"Anna!" she calls. "How many times, Anna? How *many*?"

The one named Anna remains where she is, high on the porch with her hands tipped forward, as if trying to attract a firefly. "Sweetie," the second sister says to her. "Mother's waiting. We have to go." But Anna shoos her sister off and stands perfectly still until finally the driver calls and she turns. "Jeannie Bea will have our supper," the other sister says, taking Anna by the hand and leading her down the enormous flight of steps, to the street, where the cab door is open and the girls are whooshed in with a white-gloved hand. The one goes and the other follows. They disappear behind the polish, three in a space built for two.

"You get lost in there?" Career asks. He sits on the low wall along Twentieth, shining the toes of his boots with the fist of his hand.

"Daisy was hungry."

"I guess she was."

"The girls were there. The lookalikes."

"You introduce yourself?" Career kicks off from the wall, pulls his cap tight. He squints toward the dying sun, then back at William, a crooked smile on.

96

"Course not."

"Haven't I taught you some?"

"What?"

"Some of the art of opportunity."

"I wasn't born stupid."

They walk along. The flangers and fitters, riveters and carters, chippers and caulkers gone home, and someone is baking a pie, the blueberry sugars sweet and high. Daisy strolls ahead, her ears in a perk, good as a dog already and twice as kind.

"You sit with him, then?" William asks. "Your Mr. Childs?"

"Not yet," Career says, "but he's noticed me some."

"How do you know?"

"They've moved me on."

"How do you mean?"

"From Messenger to Compositor assist. Me and Roast-Beef, both."

"Roast-Beef?"

"Another fine riser," Career says, telling William about the fifth floor of the Ledger building, and the thirty-six compositing stands and the plastered walls shellacked in oil to diminish the glare of the sun. Every compositor has his own stand, Career says, and all the type is new, and every day the news gets made, letter by letter.

"You'll be making the news, then?" William asks.

"I'm on assist."

"And Mr. Childs put you there?"

"Must have put the thought into somebody's head. Me and Roast-Beef. Temperance and industry."

"You should have another Burthey's, then," William says, pulling one from his pocket. "To celebrate."

"Crack it in two?" Career offers, taking the piece from William's hand.

"I got my own."

They walk silently, past Spring Garden, Brandywine, Green, across Mt. Vernon and Wallace. There are boys in the street, chattering girls, a metal zing, the roll of a rich cab down the street, a man on horseback. At Coates the boys turn and the prison is there—two blocks away, steeped in shadows. There's a bright streak of pink down on the horizon, stars above that, fireflies. Career pulls a pipe from his pocket and sucks the sweet of it dry, and there it is again—the rustle of bird wings.

"Your Pa hears us coming," Career says, knowing better than to ask about William's monster hunt; if there is news, he will be told. William agrees, but Daisy all of a sudden is worrying, her ears upright and her body skittish.

"What is it, girl?" William asks, but now he sees it too, a big man with a harsh stick walking a mean strut ahead. Something's wrong about him, and when Daisy bleats, Williams reels her in and scoops her up, steals inside a nearby livery stable. The buggies and surreys and cabs are stabled behind. A big coupe rockaway sits on a pile of bricks, its front axle hanging in disrepair from a low chain rack above.

"What is it?" Career asks, ducking in beside them.

"It's what I seen," William says.

"What?"

"You see it for yourself. See what I mean."

Career takes a steadying breath, then slides back out into the street. He lifts his cap, snaps it back to his head. He slides back in beside William, exhales candy breath, pipe sweetness. "Wearing a uniform," Career says.

"I know it."

William shifts Daisy into Career's arms and steps out, quiet. A gray mare deep in the stables whinnies. Career talks her out of her fuss.

"You see his face?" Career asks, when William's tucked back in.

"Like an octopus," William says, his heart pounding, his voice in a dark, nervous hush. "He turned, and I saw it."

"He see you?"

"Don't think so."

"Here," Career says. "Take her." He lifts Daisy into William's arms, steps out, stays out, uncovered, for an uncomfortable time. The mare whinnies. Career returns. "I seen it," he says. "I did." The gray features sliding around the man's face. The eyes slit straight out of the knuckle of his brow. It's as if whomever wrenched Officer Socrates Kernon together in the first place did the job on the cheap—big feet, no neck, torso like a trapezoid, face made for a monster.

"That stick a blackjack?" Career's asking.

"I reckon so."

"What's he out here for?"

"I don't know," William says. "We'll stay put. Watch him." Daisy bleats and William says shush. Daisy bleats again and William reaches into his pocket, pulls out a Burthey, lets Daisy at it.

"She eating sweets now?" Career asks.

William shrugs.

"You spoiling her rotten?"

"She's my pet, ain't she?" William asks in a hoarse whisper.

"What are you going to do?" Career asks. "About the cop?"

"Watch him first," William says, fingering the knife in his pocket. "Wasn't that the plan?"

"What good is that?" Career asks, his voice rising above the hush then quenching itself at once.

"It's all I've got so far," William says, and he can't say more, because his heart is hurting with pounding.

The light outside is falling fast, that pink streak fading. Career slips out into the dusk, then steps back in, the whites in his eyes two sudden lanterns. "Your officer's got a friend," he says.

"Who's that?"

"You look for yourself." William shifts Daisy into Career's arms; she nips at his ear. When William steps into the street all he sees is the stiff back of Kernon's dark coat and a bit of underskirt breezing in from the opposite side—ruches and frills, lavender and orange. In the deep dusk it's hard to get a proper understanding, but William stays transfixed on the scene, stealthy, struggling to hear what the two are saying a half a block down as behind him, in the livery, a mare and a stallion are turning feisty and a dog yips, awakened from sleep. Career whispers that William's been out there too long: "You're going to get noticed."

But it's the tangle of words on the street William needs to hear, the two lovers undaunted by animal sounds. Their words are private. Their distance grows—the woman's hair loose and springing, the ruches of her underskirt untamed. She puts a hand on Kernon's jacket and he pulls her near. She gives a tug to his gray, misshapen ear, laughs like it isn't the ugliest thing there is, and Kernon wraps her forcibly toward him, touches his stick to her hair. They walk a crooked line toward the river, the pink stipple in the sky all gone. A hackney cab whines west on Coates. A stray cat wanders in from the street.

"Buy me a drink," she says. "Won't you?"

"Are you proposing?"

"It's Pearl," William says, at last, stumbling back in. "Pearl from Norris." He's out of air, as if he'd given actual chase.

It takes Career a beat to understand. "The blowzy?"

William nods, catches his breath.

"I thought she was on your side. I thought. . ."

"She in it with him?" William asks. "Is she?"

"Isn't he a monster, though?" Career asks.

"Course he is. You've seen him."

William stands, confused. Daisy pushes her tongue at his chin.

"You trust a woman like that?" Career asks.

"She's a blowzy," William says, disbelieving.

"What'd you think she is?" Career, asks.

"I thought she was going to help me. I thought she said. . ." William plays the scene again in his head. Pearl learning in and laughing and Kernon touching her hair with that murdering stick, as if love were the only thing he knew, as if he had not taken that stick of his to the back of Francis's head at the crack of dawn. Crack of dying.

What have they done to my Francis?

Who did?

He's a bad man. It's proven. Like the loud release of Baldwin smoke, William's faith scatters to a nowhere place. Out in the street, the crack of horse-drawn wheels goes on past Cherry Hill, where Pa sits in the cave of his room. I'm here for you, Pa, William would say. But that's a fat lie, too, because those prison walls are much too thick, and all William's done so far is put his trust in a prostitute, out for a summer night's trick. All he's managed is to stand some in the shadows, coward-like, while the cop goes on about his business, whatever that monster's business is — thievery and murder and talking sweetness to a blowzy. William feels empty and small inside Francis's old trousers.

"I think your Pa needs a song," Career says, after a long time has passed.

William shrugs.

"You'll get the cop," Career says. "You'll know what to do."

"I'm a useless fool."

"You'll get a second turn."

"Nothing, Career. I'm just a substitute son."

"You're no substitute nothing."

"Worse than that, even."

"You didn't have your plan yet, remember? Time and a place. Industry. Patience." Career rests his arm across his best friend's back, but it doesn't bring him comfort. Daisy takes all the lead she needs.

Twenty-two

That night Francis visits William in his sleep. Comes in like he does, full of adventure. Sits down, his knees poking straight across the narrow channel of their room and pulls an arrowhead out of his pocket. It's a good luck find, he tells William, but William can hardly open his eyes to it, can't will his hand to reach across and take what Francis is offering.

"It's yours," Francis says again. "You take it."

But William can't. He can't, and Francis is fading—his big feet in Pa's old kid boots, his worn-out, faded trousers, his shirt loose at the sleeves and open at the collar. Inch by inch, Francis disappears, until only the arrowhead is floating.

When William wakes his bed is drenched with sweat. His hand is a fist—tight and empty. The earth where Francis lies buried and dead is an awful, dirty wound.

"Francis," William says out loud. "I can't do nothing."

Twenty-three

The next day William won't tell his Ma a word of it. He won't say about Pearl, about the monster, about the promise he has broken. He won't say how it is when he visits Pa at night, how it's Career who whistles up the tune, Career with his private One Thing. He won't even say about that bird. Industry and temperance, William thinks. Patience. A man needs a plan. All William has is what he'd thought to do. Take back the thing that belongs to them. Stand up to that murderer. That was the plan, but all William has is some money in Francis's trousers from a rescued heifer.

"What is it," Ma asks, "that you've been doing?"

"Rescue," he says

"It pays like you say?"

"Practically millions."

She shakes her head. She searches his eyes. She doesn't believe, anymore, in what she sees.

"You need to get out, Ma," he says. "It's time." Best he can do. Something.

She doesn't decline. She gets up slow, and she takes her time. William waits, turning the fresh coins in his pocket.

Ma has the one black dress and she wears it plainly. She ties her hair behind her ears, a messy knot. She squints at the sun when William opens the door, puts out her arm, so he can keep her steady, and all this time he doesn't say what it is he almost had last night, how he almost avenged the mad cop, Kernon. Giving Daisy the long lead, William bows like a gent. He takes the feather of Ma's arm into his hand.

"We'll go at your own speed," he says, and she nods, uncertain.

There's the heavy hoofing of horses along Callowhill, the desperate whine of hackney wheels, a couple of loose cats chasing the tail of a long, brown rat. William wears his brother's old wool trousers, which are long and heavy at the hems with dust; they are too hot. He wears his father's broke-down kid boots. He wears a shirt his Ma made him years ago. The Quinns, he thinks to himself, and he's the man of the house. When the man up ahead loses his derby hat to the breeze, William catches Ma's eye, doesn't lose hold of her arm.

"I'd forgotten," she says.

"What?"

"How crowded it is."

"You'll be fine, Ma," William says. "I'm here." Wishing he could believe what his own mouth is saying.

The machinists pull east, and north. A train squeals into a rail yard and sends a black message to the sky. A loose mutt spins on its scrawny hind legs, sniffing for scraps, and William turns and sees Molly running behind, that big bow in her streaky hair, her too-big dress buttoned on.

"Where you going?" she wants to know.

"To the market," William calls over his shoulder.

"What for?"

"Poultry," William says. "And corn. Something from the peppery-pot."

"How about some hazel nuts?" Molly asks. She's kept up her run, and now she's skipping beside them, putting her fist around Daisy's lead.

"Maybe."

"And partridge?"

William can't understand how her bow stays on. It's just dangling there on her head. "Depending on what's fresh."

"Think there'll be extras?" She drops the lead and yanks on William's sleeve. An old lady, fat and gray, gives a scolding look as she passes.

"Don't know."

"Take me with you?"

"Molly," Ma finally says, leaning across William, her voice quiet and pale, "you head on home. Your Ma will be out looking for you." Molly crosses her arms and juts out her chin.

"We'll bring you a treat," William says. "I promise." Molly's face breaks wide open with a smile. She whirls around in her sister's too-big dress, shows off the penny that she pressed to her palm.

"You go on home now," Ma says, and Molly does, running backward at first until she turns and faces west.

"She's in love with Career," William tells Ma.

"Is that right?" Ma says, smiling.

See that? William hears Francis's voice in his ear.

See what?

You saw it. You made Ma smile.

The farmers' market, when they reach it, is a foreign country. The sail of sky overhead, the long fleet of goods, the deer split into its house of ribs and the mullet come in fresh from the docks. The corn's from across the river—Burlington, Camden, Gloucester. The milk is driven in from Lancaster. The canvas bags hang from their necks, wheat bursts from its bushels, the swine sits in bloody pieces on a butcher's block. At the flower stall the sunflowers are fresh, and William buys Ma one before she can stop him.

"Don't be foolish," she says, clutching it to her heart.

He keeps his eye on her because the crowds are fierce. He worries maybe she's too thin for this, too frail. But she has fixed on a table of berries—blue and round, heart-shaped and red—and Daisy, obedient, is at her side, guarding Ma like any grown-up dog would. "A basket of each," William orders, and after that, two vendors down, a few ears of Camden corn. He buys turkey drumsticks, the feathers plucked. He buys a block of Montgomery cheese. He tells Daisy to keep minding her manners, please, buys her a treat for obeying. Sometimes, at the stalls, he makes a furtive glance for Kernon. The octopus is nowhere here. William had his chance. He's thrown it.

"You be careful," Ma says, "of that cash."

"I am."

"You won't find trouble?"

"I promise."

She studies him, pushes her hair back into its loose knot. She lets Daisy walk a circle of rope around her feet and then unwind herself again and William can't decide what Ma knows and what she guesses. What he should tell her, and when.

"Francis would want us to have pie," she decides, after a while.

"I know it."

"Just a single slice."

She stands where she is, between the berries and nuts, the flesh of her chin catching the gold engulfing tone of the sunflower and Daisy content to keep her watch. When William returns Ma is just as she was, watching the market through her big, surprised eyes and holding that flower to her chest. Daisy's chewing the loosened black threads on her hem.

"The blueberry was freshest," William says.

"Blueberry is fine."

She looks for his eyes, but he won't look for hers. They stand where they are, breaking the slice into pieces, turning their fingers sky colors. The pie is sweet and fresh and moist. Ma closes her eyes when she swallows.

"Francis would have liked that," Ma says, when she's done.

"I know he would."

"He'd be proud of you," she says, almost like a test, almost like a concession to the nearly brave. William feels a hard rising in his throat. He looks away to watch the crowds through the mist, wonders if Kernon would ever take in something sweet.

"We'll bring Molly some hazels," William says at last.

"All right."

"Take Career a pouch of tobacco."

"Go on," she says. "I got Daisy to watch."

Her pale lips are blue. Her eyes are shivers.

Twenty-four

At home they sit at the table, a bowl of berries between them and Daisy asleep at their feet. Ma pulls the green cap from each strawberry before slicing it into fours. Her fingers will carry the staining for days, and William will think, every time he sees them, of the volunteer saloon and how Ma would come home with her fingers all blued by the letters she'd write for the soldiers with her steel-tipped pen—every word she wrote and told of later expanding his idea of the country.

"Ma likes it, what she does," Francis would say when they were alone together in their room at night.

"I guess she does."

"She's good at it, too."

"Of course she is. Ma's good at it all." And she was, that is the truth. She could cook and sew and listen. She could look at you and know things. She'd probably guess at Career's One Thing, if she wanted. She could probably survive this, if only William knew how to help her.

"Something came," Ma says, and William brings this hour back into focus—the tremulous valleys of blue beneath both of Ma's eyes, the thin capillary lines that break at the bend of her nose, the small, crooked waver at the base of one eye tooth, which she broke last year and couldn't afford to fix. She fits her hand between the buttons of her dress and retrieves a page folded three times, neat. "You read it," she says. "I can't bear it."

Daisy thinks it's a present for her. Gets up from where she has been sleeping and makes a scruffy leap.

"You behave," William tells Daisy, taking the letter Ma is reaching to him from across the table and smoothing the page flat. He studies the row of words. He brings them to his face and smells them.

"Pa," he says.

"Shhh, now, Daisy," Ma says, gathering the squirmy kid to her, like the goat knows something sweet is coming and will not miss the action. "William's going to read us a story." Daisy tucks in to Ma's lap, one hoof after another. Ma feeds Daisy a strawberry cap, and after Daisy agrees with the taste of it, Ma presses a kiss between her ears and feeds her more until the caps are all gone. First Ma and then Daisy close their eyes to hear what Pa will say, from his cell at Cherry Hill.

June 30, 1871
Eastern State Penitentiary

Dearest Essie,
Dear Sons,

I keep the days in my head, and every day of all the days, I miss you.

Mornings a cart comes round and takes away the chairs we caned the day before. Cart comes around again, leaves us new caning. The wheels coming is the keeping of time, except on Sundays, Sabbath day, when Rev. John pulls his pulpit to a hearing place among the inmates and we stand, each in our own place, letting the Sabbath voice carry the distance. If it's a hymn come in with the preaching, we're allowed to sing it, and some of us do, not knowing from where the baritone comes, nor the drumming of spoons against the thick iron bars, or the wash pails, or the stools, each of us invisible to the other, but still we sing with the Sunday preaching, only some of us do. I do.

I'm good on the caning, though I will be moved on to baskets soon, which they make half a bushel to a quart measure here, cane or rattan, either, the sides fastened in to the bottom, which is turned and grooved. So long as I can still hear the wheels of the cane cart, I will make baskets, and after the baskets they are saying they will train me on segars. 150,000 a month they make here at the Hill, Pennsylvania tobacco mostly, not Spanish leaf, not anymore, and if I do fine with that, they'll send half the earning wage of it home.

That's what he said, the Visiting Inspector, spending yesterday, part of the afternoon. He promised to send you this letter. Sat with me a while, while I put my finer point upon it, writing with speed and attention. Writing missing you, my fingers split from the cane, the leftover bits of it that I turn at night, turn and fold and knot and fold until they rise up, like as on their own, into small cane creatures. I've made a donkey, a pig, a squab, a mullet so far. I've made me a 4-4-0 and an Old Ironsides, an Alexander Mitchell with its florals. Bringing them home to you, soon as I can.

I met a couple of men who came to whitewash my cell. John and William Thomas, those were the ones. Horsemen from the county.

Every once in a while a bird comes by, a mourning dove. Sits on the back wall of my exercise pen, watching me take in the sun. Sometimes at night, I think I hear a tune.

The inspector is coming round again. I'll ask him, take this letter. I'll beg on his mercy so he sends it on to you.

Loving, your husband.
Loving, your Pa

Twenty-five

"Pa's hymning," William says, after he has read the letter through four times out loud, stopping varying places each time, to give them all a chance to see it, not just William and Ma, but Daisy, too.

"Imagine," Ma says. Her voice is distant and small, and when she opens her eyes, William sees that they are swimming, the jewels in them intensified. She's started rocking Daisy, and Daisy doesn't mind. She pulls one hand down over the flop of Daisy's ear until Daisy kisses Ma with her gray-pink tongue.

"He doesn't know about Francis," she says. "He doesn't know, and how can we tell him. It'll be his final ruin."

William looks down at the letter, then back at Ma. He doesn't say what he is thinking, that the letter is dated before Francis was gone, that maybe word since has gotten in. Maybe, William thinks, Pa's already alone with the news of his son's murder. Maybe the inspector read it in the paper and passed it on, or maybe the way that mourning dove comes and sits makes Pa suspicious, or maybe it's in the sound of Career's whistle, but maybe Pa knows. Maybe it's Ma and William who don't know what Pa knows, who think time and a sentence can keep him protected.

Ma doesn't make any noise when she cries. The tears flow and Ma's eyes will wash away with the storm, if William does not save her.

"He doesn't know about the ring," Ma says. "Pa don't." It's the first she's actually spoken of it, the first she'll say what it is that the cop with the octopus face has stolen from Francis, besides his very breath and blood. Officer Socrates Kernon stole the thin slip of Ma's gold band, the words on the flesh side: *Bless our marriage, Essie.* He stole it because Francis had it, and Francis had it because he'd retrieved it just the day before from Carver W. Reed, the old pawnbroker. Francis had gone all the way to Tenth and Sansom to get Ma's piece of marriage back. Gone after Ma could not stop rubbing her naked finger to the bone, saying she'd betrayed Pa, she'd made the wrong choice, she'd put her marriage on the broker's block; couldn't Francis go?

For four days before Francis was murdered he was out on the prowl. Last day, just ahead of noon, he was in the kitchen promising William and Ma that he was bringing that ring home. "I got what it takes," he said, and neither Ma nor William asked him where he'd been or what he'd done to collect the retrieving sum, though Ma kept fitting her hand to the point of Francis's chin and brushing her cheek against his. *You're a good son, Francis.*

"I'll go with you," William had said, just as Francis was setting off for Carver Reed's. But Francis said pawnbroking was best done alone, and when William complained Francis said, "Ma needs you, and I won't be long." Last thing Francis ever said to William: *Ma needs you, and I won't be long.*

But dying is a long time, Francis. Dying is forever.

The coroner gave Ma and William an hour with Francis in the end, no more. The coroner tried to explain how it was. The bones breaking here here here, the blood in a clot at the heart, the lungs collapsing in—but all William saw was the hurt hive of his brother's head, and the bloodied trousers, loose and worn, and the lost sleeve of Francis's shirt, and the big boots with the loose tongues, and the no purse at Francis's neck, no ring. William carried his brother's brawling boots home. He carried the one-armed shirt and the sack trousers, and in every tuck and seam William searched for Ma's ring, but it was gone. Only thing William found in the bottom of a pocket was the crumple of the receipt from Carver Reed. Francis had gotten Ma's ring back, all right, and he'd died trying to save it.

"Cop thieved Francis," William said then, and as soon as he said it, he knew it was true. He knew a man as bad as a murderer of Francis had stealing Ma's wedding ring in him, too.

"It's my fault," Ma says. She thinks it still. "It's my fault that Francis is gone."

"Only the officer's fault," William tells her. "Only him that did it." And now again William thinks of the monster in his legal blues, walking the strip of road ahead of Cherry Hill, Pearl beside him and William doing nothing about it. *Nothing*. Man of the house, and a fool.

"It was me who pawned the ring," Ma says. "It was me sent Francis to fix it."

"It was the officer, Ma. You know it was."

She shakes her head no, but he's losing her again. *You see that? I saw it.* It's gone. William reads Ma's sadness in the bruised valleys beneath her eyes and the red flaring along each side of her nose, in the round of her back, her pale, taut lips. Daisy feels the sadness, too. Leaps to the floor and bleats her version.

"I think. . ." Ma says, and doesn't finish. "I think. . ." she starts again. William watches her rise. Watches her take one stair at a time, up. Hears the bedroom door close behind her, the aching deflation of the bed, the rustle of dove wings in the sky—or is that the sheets? He takes Daisy for a walk, and when they return, they find Ma damp and warm as a fever.

"I lost everything," she says, and William says, laying Daisy down beside her, "You take care of her now, Ma; the kid goat needs you."

"Where are you going?"

"You get your rest now," William says. "You take your sleep."

"You'll give Molly her hazels?"

"I will."

"You won't find trouble?"

"No, Ma. You sleep."

"Daisy's not anxious?"

"Daisy will be fine. I'll be back before dusk, Ma. I promise."

The stack of *Ledgers* is where he left it—on Ma's kitchen shelf. He takes it down and finds his page and folds it neat into his pocket. The rest of the paper he quarters back again and slips into place. "Come on, Francis," he says, and feels the ghost of his brother beside him.

Twenty-six

At the base of the bridge he hires a hackney cab and tells the driver to turn north, leaving the clanging of Bush Hill behind. The long arm of the river bends blue. The women and their children walk the paths or stare out over the world from the Water Works rail. A steamboat puffs its way up north, toward the mills that divide the river's power. William wonders if Schmitt is out there. If Francis is lying lanky on a puff of cloud stuff, watching the sculler from on high.

You think Schmitt'll take it, Francis?

I know he will.

In his mind, to his dead brother, William confesses. *Had Kernon in my sights,* he says, *and then I lost him. Could have asked him for Ma's band, does he still have it. Could have, Francis. I should have.* In the hackney cab, there is no consolation. In the horse that pulls and the driver that directs him, there is silence only, and beyond the cab, the flat-bottomed anthracite boats and the team boats and the rowers keep moving, and the river keeps bending north, toward the millworks of Manayunk. 87 Maiden Lane, William had told the driver, home of Dr. Radway.

You sure of it? Francis might as well ask William.

I'm sure of nothing, Francis.

In the fold of the *Ledger* is the story William's trusting, the promise that Dr. Radway has been making. It's the miracle story of the Sarsaparilla Resolvent, one dollar a bottle, five dollars for six—the women under its spell in a proven revival. William unfolds the paper and reads it again, studying the picture of the heroine first, then reading the type beneath:

The subject of the above Likeness Is at present one of the most Intelligent, brilliant, and beautiful ladies of this metropolis, in the full enjoyment of redolent health, vigorous life and strength, dispensing charity to the needy, consolation and attendance to the sick, devoting her leisure hours to assisting the poor and distressed, and contributing to their necessities.

This lady was rescued from a miserable existence through the instrumentality of Dr. Radway's Resolvent.

It's just what Ma needs—those things precisely. Redolent health. Vigorous life. Strength. The proven Dr. Radway's Resolvent. William is not Pa. William could never be Francis. He is only who he is—a boy without a better plan and with a Ma who needs something more than he is, if anything can cure her. *I saw Kernon,* he should have told her, but he didn't. *I saw him with my own eyes, the thief of Francis, and I did nothing.* What good is honesty if the truth is helpless? What good is the second son when the first is buried in a pauper's hill?

"We'll mark the grave," Ma had whispered. "When we're ready."

They wouldn't be ready.

"87 Maiden Lane?" the driver calls back, wiping a bead of sweat just before it funnels deep down into his collar. They've crossed a canal bridge, headed up a narrow road. The smell of Manayunk is wool and cotton.

"Yes, sir."

"You want me to wait on you, then?"

"If you could."

"I'll be taking Trinket around for a bucket of water. Be done in a half hour."

"Sir."

"You meet me here, and you don't be late, or we'll be adding to your fare, you hear me?"

"I hear you, Mister. I'm indebted."

The street is narrow, the houses tight. It's Dr. Radway himself who opens the door—a tall man with a thick beard who looks William up and down before he speaks.

"You here for the cure?" he asks, and William nods vaguely.

"One bottle or six?"

"Six," William says. "It's for my mother."

Inside the house is roots and vine. A bowl of tiny berries. "Your Ma have trouble with her liver, son?"

"No, sir."

"Her complexion confounded?"

"Not her complexion, complexion's fine."

123

"Her blood in want of cleansing? Her kidney in trouble?"

"It's neither of those things, doctor."

"What is it you are asking for, then?"

"My Ma's heart is broke," William says. "And I can't fix it."

Twenty-seven

He mixes the medicine in with Ma's tea and carries the cup and its saucer, that chunk of Montgomery cheese and its plate up the stairs to her room, where the only sun that still shines sits on the sill.

"Ma," William says, entering in. "I made you something."

Halfway across the floor, looking up, he stops short. There are three in the bed, not two, and only one of them an animal.

"Molly?" he asks. "Whatever are you. . ."

The girl shoots up like a lightning strike, yanks at the tent of her skirt and the mess of her un-bowed hair. Daisy, long against Molly's thigh, perks too—shakes her head like she's ridding it of dreams.

"You sure were a long time coming," Molly says, as if she has any business being here, any reason to judge. Ma turns from her side to her back, opens one eye.

"William?" she asks, sleepily.

"Ma? Molly?"

Daisy's the first on her feet. Scrambles down from the edge of the bed and William sees how the kid is wearing Molly's flopping bow, the yellow silk around her neck, the lead roped into it. Like a circus goat, William thinks, casting a strong, censuring eye on Molly, but Molly just stares back like the yellow ribbon is a wise replacement and maybe, William thinks, it is. He leaves it be.

"What are you doing here, Molly?" William asks.

"Hazel nuts," she says. "You promised."

"You helped yourself in? Just like that?"

"I knocked first, didn't I, Mrs. Quinn? I knocked, and I heard a *Come in.*"

"Ma?" William asks.

"It's all right, son. It's fine."

Daisy gets onto her back legs, wanting up. William lays the saucer and the cheese plate down on the bedside table and takes the kid into his arms. She licks the salt sweat from his neck and chin. "She's hungry," William says, and Molly says, "Of course she is. Where have you been?"

"Business."

William lays Daisy back down onto Molly's lap, collects the tea and cheese, and walks around to Ma's side of the bed. Without even asking, Molly leans in—lifts Ma's head and stuffs her pillow until she's practically upright.

"Drink your tea, Ma. Drink it up."

Molly helps William with the serving—holds the saucer while he holds the cup and hardly fidgets. Nobody talks until some tea is swallowed down, until Ma says it's enough now, please let her sleep, and William insists on more tea.

126

"I'm just so tired."

"For your strength, Ma," William says, and Molly's reaching in with the wedge of cheese, and breaking it gentle, and William sees how she waits on Ma, feeds her the cheese, doesn't take her eyes away until Ma swallows, and suddenly William doesn't mind so much that Molly's been lying here this afternoon, making three with Daisy and Ma.

"Did you get your hazel nuts, then?" he asks her.

Molly shakes her head a disappointed no. "Your ma didn't know where they was put."

"They're in the spice jar," William says, "by the sink."

"All right."

"Bought enough of them for you to share."

"I like hazel nuts," she says. "I like 'em enough to eat them all on my own." She shifts Daisy from her lap to the sheets of the bed and scoots out of the room, down the stairs. William hears her now, shuffling the things out of their places. Finally he hears the sound of a cap being unscrewed.

"Have some more tea, Ma," William says.

She drinks a little. "You were gone a long time."

"I know it."

"Career came and went."

"So early?"

"Said he had news. Said he'll meet you at Preston."

"All right."

127

"Preston is for mothers and their babies, William. What business do two boys have at Preston?"

"We like the garden," William says.

"The garden?" She looks at him hard, searches for a real answer, decides not to pursue it and sighs. Now it's William searching his mother's eyes for signs of a healing heart. The shadows in the valleys of her face are purple-gray. The lines of red at the base of her nose don't seem to be so angry.

"You'll be okay?" he asks.

She sighs again, doesn't answer.

"Weren't your fault, Ma, what happened."

"Don't make me a liar, William. At least."

"I wouldn't."

"I know what's honest."

She drinks a little more tea, and William sits with her silent. He remembers Dr. Radway's words. Redolent health. Vigorous life. Strength. He checks her face for signs.

"Career's waiting," Ma says, "and I told him you'd come. You go along, take Molly with you."

"Molly?"

"She's been tending to me all afternoon long."

"But, Ma. . ."

"And bring Daisy, too. I'll take my sleep in the meanwhile." She straightens the mounded pillow at her back and flattens herself to it. She closes her eyes and William studies her face. No sign yet of the Resolvent. It could be another sham. Another wrong choice. These days are full of them.

"Come on now, Daisy," William says after a while, and the kid stands at once, perks her ears straight. She looks funny in her yellow bow. Funny, but maybe also elegant.

Twenty-eight

Molly doesn't have quiet in her. She doesn't know what it would be just to walk and not talk, and after a spell, William is only partway listening to the rat-a-tat of Molly's stories about her Pa, a machine man, and her Ma in the service of five sons, two daughters, and a baby who won't stop either hollering or complaining. Molly rations out the hazel nuts as she goes. Sucks the salt off of them first, then chomps down hard, so that her words are full of nut bits and sometimes, after she swallows, the parts are still sitting there, in the crease of her lips and on her tongue.

"Yellow does Daisy good, don't you think?" she's asking.

"I guess it does."

"See how she walks, proud to show her necklace off?"

"I think she's hungry," William says. "Hungry and knows the way to Preston." He says it, then regrets it, but Molly doesn't bother.

"Career will be surprised," Molly says.

"He sure will be."

"He won't expect to see me, but I'll be here."

"Yes, Molly."

"I brought my penny," she says, tapping her skirt pocket. "He'll teach me toss."

"Depends on other things."

130

"Like what?"

"I don't know, Molly. Just does."

She looks up at William and shakes her head, like she's sorry for his lack of knowing. "I like how Career is," she offers. "And I also like how handsome. He has a future, and everybody sees it. I see it best of all." She nods her head once, fast, for emphasis, and William, despite himself, despite everything, smiles.

There is heat on the tracks where they cross them—the furnace of the day and of the trains gone by. William looks up and down the rails to the changeable horizon lines. Another two hours of light, he figures, and so much to do in between.

"You sure you're not tired?" he asks Molly.

"I'm sure."

"Your feet aren't sore?"

"My feet are never sore."

Daisy pulls ahead, and Molly skips behind. William lengthens his stride to keep up, tips his head to passersby, looks into the shadows of things. Two tomcats face off across an alley and a white bird flies. The fringe tail of a setter slaps the ragged hem of the sky.

"I see him!" Molly calls out, and now she's running, and suddenly Daisy is trying to keep up from behind, squeaking as she gallops. The polish of Career's boots is collecting the low sun. He puffs a cloud of pipe smoke. He's been sitting on the Preston wall, but now he stands, squinting his eyes in William's direction.

"What's this?" he asks.

"We've come for you," Molly answers. She stops just short of the wall, and Daisy stops, too. William is there in no time. Career has exchanged his cranberry vest for a silver one. His jacket is slung across one shoulder.

"It's your receiving party," William says.

"I didn't know I called on one."

"Molly's been helping Ma this afternoon."

"And where were you?"

"Out on business."

Career whistles low. He has his secrets, and William has his. The One Thing. The everything. The search for a cure.

"Ma says you stopped by," William says, after Career has had a chance to hold his judgment.

"I did."

"What for?"

William waits and Molly looks up, her face the gleam of expectation. Career looks from her to William to Daisy again. "You take Daisy into the garden," Career tells her.

"Right now?" It's like someone took Molly's face and crushed it — her brown-gold eyes and her freckles fold; her mouth is a thin, unhappy squeeze.

"Daisy's hungry, isn't she, Molly? And don't you have her lead?"

"I guess so."

"It would be the biggest help to us, Molly," Career says, bending toward her, putting a hand on Daisy's head. "Honest, it would. And you've done such a nice job already with the kid, putting her into that fresh collar of hers."

Molly's face brightens. "You mean it?"

"I do."

"You teach me toss afterwards?"

"Tomorrow," he says, "when the sun returns." Molly stares at Career to gauge his truthfulness. She makes her decision and leads Daisy off, but not before Career has warned her to be careful. "Daisy will eat the whole place, if you let her," he says. "You temper her appetite, take cautions." Molly listens hard, blows Career a kiss, then Daisy and Molly disappear into the garden.

"What were you thinking," Career asks, "bringing her along?"

"It was Ma who insisted."

"What was your Ma thinking, then?"

"Ma isn't well," William says. "Don't you remember?"

Career sucks on his pipe and gets it going again. He closes his eyes and exhales. He takes a seat on the wall and William sits down beside him. "Your lookalikes were here and gone," he finally says.

William turns, looks over his shoulder. "What were they doing?"

"Same as usual. Goodwill call. Philanthropy and charity. The privilege of the rich."

William shrugs. There's nothing for it. He looks at Career in his silver vest and his combed black hair and that dimple in his chin and thinks about what Molly said: He has a future. "Ma said you had news," he reminds him.

Career studies William's face, then nods. He slips his hand into his vest and retrieves a single page from the *Public Ledger* all creased into a portable square. He unfolds it out of its careful wedge, until the story he wants is laid out flat on William's lap.

"What?" William asks.

"Tomorrow's paper," Career says.

William holds the page to the dying light and scans until he sees it.

LOCAL AFFAIRS.

THE FRANCIS QUINN HOMICIDE CASE——CORONER'S INVESTIGATION——Yesterday morning Coroner Goddard held an investigation into the circumstances connected with the death of Francis Quinn, aged 21 years old and who resided on Carleton Street. The deceased died at the House of Corrections on 1st of July, from the effects of a beating received in the rear of No. 410 Hagner Street, at the hands of Policeman Socrates F. Kernon, just previous to his commitment by Magistrate McClintock.

Dr. Wolford, the Coroner's Physician, made a post mortem examination of deceased, and he testified that he found the body much decomposed. He examined the head and face, and found the right side of the nose badly fractured, and there was a cut on the head; the scalp was opened and a number of bruises were found, but there was no fracture of the skull and no effusion of blood on the brain. Death was caused by violence of some kind, and would result from a number of blows from a man's fist. The injuries resembled blows from a blackjack, and the condition of the body showed that deceased was of intemperate habits.

Rebecca Craig, 410 Hagner street, testified that she knew the deceased. He came to her house, and the last time was 2 A.M.; he went to sleep in a shed in the yard, and witness heard him there snoring. He came into the yard by way of the gate, and he was in the habit of sleeping in the shed in the yard. A policeman came into the yard between five and six o'clock, and pounded Quinn badly, and witness heard Mary King say that a man was beating Francis. Witness went out and heard the officer say "I've got it in for you anyhow." Quinn was bleeding at the nose and did not attempt to fight the officer. The officer struck Quinn twice. Witness told the officer not to take Quinn, and the latter said, "Don't hit me, you'll fetch back the hemorrhage on me." Quinn was beaten by the officer for about fifteen minutes and witness heard a scuffle in the alley after Quinn was pulled out by the officer. Witness recognizes the officer. Witness heard the officer say "You've got to go if I kill you."

Mary King, residing with the last witness, testified that she saw Quinn every day; he always slept in the shed, and the last time he was there she heard a man was being beaten and heard Quinn's voice, heard a man say "Get out of here" and then Quinn said, "I've got a right here;" witness then heard several heavy blows, and Quinn said, "You're not going to take me, are you? I've done nothing;" the officer then beat him about the head and deceased was bleeding dreadfully; the officer would not give the deceased time to wash off the blood. and dragged Quinn and dragged him on the pavement and beat him with his fist; Quinn said, "You might as well kill me at once," and then the officer put the nippers on him and dragged him.

John M. Anderson reported that he saw the beating and heard the officer say, "I've got it in for you and I'll kill you;" Quinn said, "Well kill me then;" the officer then struck Quinn with his fist and the nose later bled and the officer would not give him time to wash the blood away.

Moses Jones said that he was turnkey at the Nineteenth District Station House; Quinn was brought into the station house about 6 A.M. Wednesday two weeks ago, very drunk, but he had no blood on him; he was put in a cell and lay down on the floor and remained there until the Magistrate heard his case: Quinn made no complaint against the officer at the station house.

Major Oliver, Assistant Superintendent of the House of Corrections, reported to Quinn's admittance to the House of Corrections. His eye was black but there was no blood.

Another individual, name undisclosed, said that Quinn had said he received his black eye through being kicked by a horse.

A further investigation and possible sentencing of Officer Socrates Kernon is pending.

Twenty-nine

William hears his heart in his ears, can't stop his hands from trembling. He reads the words again in the dying light, the sorrowing story, and turns to Career, his stomach sickened.

"Worse thing possible," he says, and Career says, "I know it."

"He asked for his life, and it weren't given."

Career agrees, solemn and sad, his face momentarily veiled by a puff of pipe smoke.

"They're calling Francis an intemperate."

"I asked," Career says, "if they wouldn't say it. I asked at the desk, when they were putting the type in, but the news is the news, and they report it."

"He did not attempt to fight," William says, reciting from the *Ledger.*

"That's one of them, anyway, with the story."

"You think Francis would have said that?"

"What?"

"*Well kill me then.* With Ma at home and Pa in jail and me his brother? Would he have asked for his own killing?"

"Course not. He was Francis."

"Why'd they put it there, then? In your own *Ledger*, coming to newsstands tomorrow?"

Career slips the paper from William's lap and folds it back into its squares. "It's reporting," Career reminds him. "Like I said. You have to keep your focus now. You're the man of the house. Your Ma's depending."

"Focus on what?" William's head throbs. His eyes hurt. The fireflies have come out into the night, and not one of them is in focus; it's just all blurred light. The Kunkle hasn't worked and maybe the Resolvent won't work, either. Whatever Career thinks William has in him is likely just more shamming.

"They could take Kernon from the street when this is done," Career says, turning to put his hand on William's shoulder, to help him see. "They take him before you get to him, and you'll never get back your Ma's gold ring. You'll never get your chance at it, William, and then what is there left to you? Nothing."

"He's a monster," William says.

"I know what he is."

"A lying thief of a man."

"Your Ma's ring isn't his to have."

"He split him and Francis was sleeping."

"I see it, William. I know it." From behind them, past the wall of trees, there is the sound of babies mewling, the sound of mothers singing, the sound of a white goat in a garden, Molly's low whispers beckoning, calling.

138

"It wasn't no horse that kicked him," William says, quieting his voice, steadying the shake of his hands, glancing back quick, over his shoulder. "I know that for sure. And he liked his drink is all, not a crime in it. And none of this would have happened, besides, if Frank Doyle hadn't wanted the extras for his son. It's one misfortune leading to another, Career, and look what it is, how they tell it, in the paper."

"What's done is," Career says. "What's next is up to us. Think of your Ma, William. How the ring coming home would lessen the sorrow."

"I saw Kernon and I was a coward, Career. I saw him, and I stayed hid. You was there. You know it."

"You'll have your second chance, you'll take it."

"How do you know second chances are coming? How do you know I'm up to it?"

"I ain't stupid," Career says. "I don't go choosing cowards as my only best friend." He stares into William with the coals of his eyes. He fits his hand firm around William's worn collar. He's got ink on his face, just below the left eye. The silver of his vest shines bright.

"My only line to him is Pearl, and looks like Pearl's his lover," William says, glancing back over his shoulder again, because Molly's coming, pulling at Daisy through the shadows.

"Maybe she ain't."

"You saw it."

"Maybe she was working on your behalf."

139

"Now what would she do that for?"

"She fed you, didn't she?"

"I guess maybe."

"Two times you went to the bar and two times you were fed. And she listened to your story, William. You told me that she did."

"I guess it."

"Time is slipping," Career says. "You go on. I'll take Molly and that kid goat back home."

Thirty

William leans against the streetlamp, corner of Broad and Pennsylvania, the light an apron of yellow around his old, broke boots. Two brown moths flap at his head, fuzzy creatures with gigantic wings that make him think of the night he and Francis and Ma sat within the spectacle of the Phasmatrope. She'd caught her breath as soon as the first projected waltz had begun, and by the time the tumblers started galvanizing and leaping across the screen, Ma was pulled to the edge of her seat, her sons on either side each holding one hand. Ma's fingers were white from the laundry bleach. Her nails were short and square. It was her gold ring that shone like a star that night, an infinity band. William remembers remembering Pa and what Pa'd been through and what he'd done and lost, and how the bearing of him had changed, but never his outright love for Ma.

"You did right," William said to Francis, late that night when they got home—had walked the city, three astride, the one near the other keeping safe and warm in the winter chill.

"Did you see how she looked?" Francis asked, lying with his knees bent in his bed.

"I did."

"Pretty as a song, William. You write it to Pa. You tell what we've done."

"I'll tell him you bought the tickets fair."

"Tell him what you want."

"He'll know what I mean, whatever I write him."

"Just tell him about Ma."

Now William wishes more than anything that he could talk to Pa, that Pa still went to Matthias Baldwin's yard each day and came home talking about the five thousand parts each of a leading locomotive, the pieceworks and standards, the interchangeables and their instruction cards, the men like Edward Longstreth, friend of Pa's, an apprentice machinist who rose up the ranks to machining foreman and erecting foreman and general superintendent. "There's democracy in the machines," Pa would say. "There's freedom." *Sometimes at night, I think I hear a tune.*

There are carriages and hackneys in the streets, steam up above, moon on the rails. William looks up and waits for the mourning dove—looks for her in the high bell tower, but for the moment, in this mission, William is alone, the bird elsewhere on its soar to somewhere. An hour ago, maybe less, William asked for Pearl over the burnished bar and Thomas said she hadn't come in yet, best to wait for her outside, and while Thomas was talking, and then Bryant chiming in, Jerry had come around quick to say that if it was oysters William wanted he could have them for him quick.

"Waiting on Pearl," William had said. "But I thank you for the offer."

It's summer but a breeze has come in. It's late but there's still the echo of machines in the air. The door of the Norris House cranks wide and a

143

man pushes through, short and wide, his trousers too long and his vest too bright along the stripes. He carries a top hat in his hands, as if he's just finished with a show or going to make one, and behind him trail two women, skinny and crooked as sticks. When they turn and see William at the post, they bow. They tell him the action is where they're headed for, if he wants to come along.

"No thank you, sir. Ma'ams."

"You sure, son?"

"I am."

It's a busy night at Norris: bands of revelers strutting in and leaking out. As William stands within the lamplight, a crowd rumbles in from behind—picks its way toward Norris between the carriages and hackney cabs of Broad, yanks at the door, and falls in, while at the same time the old man who wears the news on his head falls out, and, just behind him an unfamiliar older lady, the shine of the light catching the white hairs along her lip. They stop for a long time and blink at the night. When the man turns west, toward the Schuylkill, the woman does, too, catching her hand in his for balance and reminding William of Career and Molly an hour, maybe two hours before, starting off for home—Molly reaching her hand toward Career's, and Career taking it but only as a precaution against the dark. "Daisy's a good kid," William had heard Molly saying, and he wonders how it was, in their long walk home, and he wonders how it is now, for Molly in her house of too many brothers, for Daisy and Ma, side by side, for Career, on his way to tomorrow's news, his One Thing still staked up, secret.

The pain inside thickens. The doubts are at him. He needs Pearl's help. He wants to trust her.

He checks the sky again for the bird, but it's moon and stars. He holds his hand over his own heart, and his heart is a mess, fanatically pumping. He digs deep into his pocket for the second bottle of Dr. Radway's Sarsaparilla Resolvent—*Redolent health. Vigorous life. Strength.*—and turns it over and over in his hands, considering, weighing, until finally he turns the cap and by the light of the moon and stars, the tall streetlamp, he tosses half the tincture back and waits for his soul to cure, his courage to gather.

Finally, from behind, on Broad, William hears a hackney cab squeal to a sudden stop. He hears the quick snap of a brusque shout, the crash of overskirts and lace, the nasty slap of whip crack, and then, just as fast, the horse pulls off, tipping onto its back hooves and up before the driver has it back in its charge. The speed of its escape pounds hard into the street. A terrible rumple is left in the road, a mangle of person and skirts.

"Ma'am?" William asks, hurrying out onto Broad Street, toward her. "Ma'am, you all right, there?"

He leans in, puts his hand down to reach for hers, and he's the only one who does, the only one on all of Broad who has the honor in him. The victim smells like the inside of a pub. Her hair is loose and wild. Her shoes are slippers, not proper boots, and when she turns, when she lifts her face toward his, he sees the roundness of her eyes and a hurt shoots through him.

"Pearl," he says. "What happened?"

He crouches close. She doesn't move. He looks for an easing way to help her. He doesn't know what might be broke and what might worse than hurt her. When he puts his hands beneath her head, she catches her breath—a sharp intake of air. Slow as anything he's ever seen, she lifts her hands to her hair to unpin the ruined knot. She wipes at the skin beneath one eye and reveals a black bruise there.

"Pearl," William says. "That you?" A small crowd has gathered, but it keeps its distance. No one has called for any help, no one asks for a doctor or a stretcher or some whiskey, because for women like Pearl they never do. The cab drivers keep their horses to the other side of Broad. William feels a slight disturbance by his head—those moths of his, come to hover.

"Help me," Pearl says, but barely, her voice a hoarse whisper. "Can you?"

"Can you stand?"

"I'm going to try it." She pushes to her knees, unsteady. She pushes to standing, and it's worse. She stumbles, but William's there to catch her. She stands unsteady in a low crouch, then stands up taller. When she lifts her hands again to fix her hair, William sees a long tear down her sleeve.

"William," she says, her voice as hurt as the rest of her.

146

"What happened to you?"

"It's that officer of yours," she says, her words all wrong and scrambled, her breath in pieces. "Mean as a crab in a trap."

"What did he hurt you for?"

"Come on," she whispers. "Get me out of here. There's things your Ma should know."

Thirty-one

They take the narrow streets home, the darkest ones, her bruises changing colors with the night. *Mean as a crab in a trap.* Every time she lifts her hand to the yarn of her hair, her sleeve rips harder, and when she walks she struggles for her balance. She stops and leans into the shadow of the machines, dodging the fraction of moonlight.

"I'll fetch you a doctor, ma'am," William says.

"I'll be fine." But it's as if her words have been battered, too—masticated, crumbled.

"I can pay."

"Don't you be foolish."

Her vowels are a single sore sound. She won't tell him what she knows or what she has. It's William's Ma she wants to see, that's what she tells him, but home's a distance. Pearl will get a long block in and stop, her breath coming hard, her hand on that patch of her dress where a rusty stain has set in. She will start again and then she can't—slides her back down the rough face of a high brick wall and sits hugging her knees to her chin. She rocks slow slow slow, and when she breathes again, she rattles. She works something around to the front of her mouth and spits out the cracked half of a tooth.

"Ma'am," William crouches. "Ma'am?" Her face, in the shatters of the moonlight, is honest and naked. Without her lipstick and rouge, she looks young enough to be Ma's daughter—her eyes with that touch of violet to them and her bottom lip swollen. She pushes another fraction of tooth to the surface and holds the white split between a finger and thumb, then drops it between them to the street. When she tugs the clip from the back of her head, her hair tumbles to her waist. There's a row of corkscrews along the edge, the sort that one presses in for a child.

"You ever hear of Dr. Radway's Resolvent?" William asks, after a rat hurries past and they watch it go and she says nothing. It's like's she's half-asleep, or maybe half dead, and William digs into the well of Francis's trouser pocket and retrieves the bottle. He holds it up to the quarter moon and it's still there, the last drops of sarsaparilla.

"Might do you good," he says, and she doesn't fight it, stares straight past him. He unscrews the cap, lifts the bottle to her, gentle and delicate around her swelling. "Give it some time," he says. "Let it work its powers." But it takes her a long, long time to swallow, as if she couldn't, for a moment, remember how.

They sit and they watch the light in the black beans of the rat's eyes, its tail swatting around at the gutter. They sit and they don't talk and William doesn't ask and from the west end of the wall, a dog wanders in, red and white with a fringe. William makes it out to be that setter from the classifieds.

"He's a lost boy," William says.

"You know him?"

"Only just lately seen him."

They watch it scoot back and forth, one side of the street to the other, its tail brooming between its back legs, its nose low. It keeps one ear up, its shoulders high. It's hungry for a scrap, but it finds nothing.

"I had a dog once," Pearl finally says over her ripe lip.

"That's nice."

"I had a husband, too, until things went sour."

William doesn't know what to make of it, doesn't look for a solution. The rat is gone; the dog is pacing. "Boy," William finally calls, and the setter's tail picks up, its nose needles around in his direction, its tongue droops over a row of jagged teeth. The setter barks three sharp notes, lifts a front foot. Then he moans, bows down, a midnight supplicant.

"There's no accounting for a bad man," Pearl says, and William turns toward the split plum of her lip, her faucet eyes, and knows for certain that he'll never confess his own spying, the things he'd seen over by Cherry Hill, the things he thought and said: *Just a flat-out, nothing-of-good-to-her blowzy.* Something's happened, and it's Ma she wants to see, Ma he has to get her to, and still they wait on the Resolvent.

"It's only six blocks more," William finally says, and Pearl nods. "You think the strength is in you?"

150

She gives him her hand and he helps her to her feet. She stands there, catching her balance. "Look," she garbles, as the setter circles near.

William reaches a hand toward the dog and makes him promise: "You be good, you hear? You be respectful." The dog yips a little, works its tongue across William's fingers. "You must be Spank," William says to the dog, "Spank's your name now, isn't it?" He holds out his hand and the setter agrees, grateful for his name in the mouth of a good stranger.

Thirty-two

Daisy has gone from Ma's arms to William's, taken an indignant nip at his ear. Beyond Ma, in the window, day is breaking. There's the shadow of a stir, a dove's song, a machine being whirred into full throttle, a tomcat howl. Ma has tied her hair back into a knot, thrown on a carmine-colored dress, collected a green shawl about herself (though it is the first of August and by noon she will be looking for a fan). *You can't*, she has said. *You won't.* Over. Again. *You can't stay out all night. You won't leave me to my worry. You can't know what it is until you have children of your own. Until you lose one.*

"A night prowler," she says. "Like your brother Francis. That's what you'll be, William. That's what you're becoming."

"No, ma'am."

"I raised you different. "

"I wasn't. . ."

"All night, William. The whole smoky darkness of it and me thinking something had happened to you, too."

"I didn't mean it, Ma."

"I went next door," she says, "and asked Mrs. May. I went down and asked your Molly. Nobody knew, William."

"You did that, Ma? On your own you did?"

"You were gone, William. Like your brother. Leaving me to Daisy."

"I wanted to tell you, Ma."

"It's trouble, isn't it, William. It's more Quinn trouble. Might as well tell me." There's a fire to her, a fierceness he had thought was permanently gone.

"It's not like you think it is."

"What do I think it is? You and Career over at Preston Retreat. You staying out and coming home smelling like taverns. You putting coins ahead of us, and not saying where they've come from?"

"I thought you'd be sleeping, see? Like you've been, Ma. You've been sleeping. Nights before this, you. . ."

"I lost Francis," she says, her eyes filling, her face in a high, agitated flush, "and for four years more, counting from now, your Pa is lost. Do not ask me, William Quinn, to account for my sadness." There's a flutter of noise downstairs, a yip, but Ma doesn't seem to notice. Ma's eyes are on him, her whole attention, and for the first time he can think of, William is glad for the intensity of her anger. *Redolent health. Vigorous life. Strength.*

"I should have told you," he says, and downstairs, again, there's the crackle of something, a clattering of sharp nails on floorboards, and if Ma hears it, her face doesn't let on.

"I won't lose you, William. I will not. I refuse it."

He feels a clutch in his heart. He lets Daisy wriggle free. He watches the kid walk a nervous circle between himself and Ma, until finally Daisy

153

leaves the two of them to one another and gambols out the bedroom door and toward the narrow echo of the stairs and down. Before William has the chance to think of it, to stop it, the riot begins: Spank in an almighty clamor of bark talk and Daisy in a spit, full of territory and terror, and Pearl talking in her ruined way, her words all marbles: "You be good like William asked you. Don't you mind that kid goat now, Spank. You remember yourself." But Spank won't, and Daisy is a Quinn, and now Ma's behind William on the stairs, calling to Daisy until the goat loses her courage and turns—up the stairs, past William to Ma, who pulls the goat's bewilderment into the chaos of her own, and even if Francis were standing right here beside him, William would not know where to begin.

"Just what kind of trouble are you in?" Ma asks at last, her voice trembling. "*Precisely?*"

William steps down and Pearl stands and the dog heels. The day's sun streams in. Ma gets Daisy to chatter down until they are here, on the first floor in the front room, the machines down the way and Pa on the Hill, and Ma staring at Pearl, and William between them. "I was getting myself around to the introductions," William says, finally.

"*Introductions*, William?"

"To Pearl, Ma," he says, then: "Ma, here's Pearl."

"I'll need better than that, William." Daisy struggles at her shoulder, but Ma holds firm. Her hair is loose and eyes are alive. She's taking her survey of Pearl.

154

"Pearl's a friend," William says. "I brought her home."

"I see."

"The dog's a lost and found."

"Is that right?"

"It is."

"And so you've brought them here."

William nods.

"The result of your night travels."

"There's a story to it."

"I imagine so."

"It was me," Pearl intervenes, her vowels still sore and her lip worse than before. "I was the one asking the boy to bring me here."

"I'm not much of a boy, ma'am," William defends himself.

"You're boy enough," Ma says. She looks from William to Pearl, from Pearl to William. She does what she can to divine their business and then gives up the battle. She puts her hand on Daisy's head. The kid settles against the green fringe on her shoulder.

"Pearl's been helping me," William says.

"Has she now?"

"And now she's come to talk to you."

"Whatever for?"

"You'll have to ask Pearl for yourself, Ma. I asked her, but she wouldn't tell me." Ma steps forward, lifts one hand to her hair. She tells Daisy to be a good goat now, and then she stands, deciding.

"This is a strange business, William."

"I admit it."

"That is no comfort, the way I see it."

"I guess maybe it won't be."

Pearl looks like she might talk, but doesn't. She wobbles back and forth on her unsteady legs, her hair in that mess of a nest and her dress torn and the rust stain ugly with the dawn. Ma's eyes take it in but cannot calculate, until finally Daisy starts bleating again and the red and white barks and Ma tells them both, please, to be quiet.

"I need to know what this is," Ma finally says. "I need the beginning first, and then the thing Pearl's come for."

"If I could talk to you alone, ma'am," Pearl manages. "Please." She's wobbling worse than before, and Spank barks bright in her defense, and William's the one to catch her, to settle her down in a chair by the table, the smell of her still hot and hurting. Ma runs the kid upstairs and closes the bedroom door. She returns with a can of salts from her volunteering days, a rag and a bowl for some water.

"Pearl?" she asks, and Pearl says, "He hurt me."

"*Who* hurt you?" Ma asks, spinning on her heel and glaring at William, as if he had this in him, too, the beating of a Norris House blowzy.

"The officer," Pearl says, and Ma says, "You need to tell me."

"Your son's a good boy," Pearl says.

"I know it," Ma agrees, reluctant.

"I need us alone," Pearl says, "if you please," and Ma's at the sink getting water, filling the kettle, setting it to boil, and Pearl sets her head on the table to rest and Spank whines, as if he failed to save them all, and William looks again at Ma and knows the Resolvent is working through her, and if it is, then, if it is, could the stuff be alive in him, too?

"You have business," Ma asks William, "with that dog?"

"Yes, ma'am."

"You get yourself to it, then. We'll talk your part in all this later."

Thirty-three

There are thirty dollars in his pocket when he returns. Daisy greets him at the door like a proper pup. The sun coming in through Ma's kitchen window is the color of humidity and fog, a white cast against which Ma's dress steeps a deeper red. She looks up at William from across the table, where she sits facing Pearl, then returns her attention to Pearl's spoiled dress, the lavender and orange spill between them.

Pearl's hair is a gloss of brushed gold, a bolt of silk that falls down her back, and when she turns toward William, he understands that she's put Ma's old navy blue and white dress on, that uniform from the Volunteer days with the union emblem sewn up high into its neck. The bruises along Pearl's jaw are brightening with the sun. The plum of her lower lip has darkened to maroon. But it's Pearl's eyes that William sees most clear, above the blue of Ma's uniform. *She's pretty,* he thinks, and then, after that, *Francis might have loved her.* And after that, *She is no blowzy.*

"You get your business done?" Ma asks him. She turns Pearl's split sleeve inside out and wets the tail end of a thread with her lips and won't look directly at him, won't let on just what has happened here, or where she stands with him.

"Yes, ma'am."

"You worked up a hunger?"

He nods.

"Mrs. May has brought us some pie," she says, fitting the thread through the eye of the needle and nodding its end. "We left you a slice. Peach."

He carries Daisy to the table and sets her at his mother's feet. He takes the slice of pie from a shelf near Ma, and Ma's right: it's fresh, it's sweet. He eats until there's nothing but shine on his plate and Ma's finished a neat row of stitches, and he takes the plate away and digs down into Francis's pocket and spreads out the coins from his find. Ma's eyes widen but she doesn't speak, and William thinks of those days of the Volunteer Saloon, when Ma would come home talking about strangers and purpose. He thinks about the days before losing Francis, when Ma sat here, her eyes down and her hands busy and her heart anxious, but alive like this. She says nothing about the coins. He leaves them in a stack.

Ma sews and Daisy snores and Pearl watches. There's the sound of the thread pulling through, the machines outside, the huffing and whirring. Ma says little things and Pearl says nothing until finally Pearl breaks the near silence.

"I told your Ma," she says, "what I had to."

William looks from the violet of Pearl's eyes to the emeralds of Ma's and waits, but that's it for now, all they're telling. Suddenly William understands that what has been said belongs to them, and what has been done has been talked through and forgiven, secrets being the providence of

159

women, the sheltering of shame and heartbreak. William thinks of Officer Kernon at Cherry Hill. He thinks of Pearl, and of himself, a coward in the shadows. He waits for Ma or Pearl to explain what happened next, but neither one is so inclined.

"Your ma," Pearl says at last. "She misses Francis."

He nods.

"It's a hard business, missing is."

"I know it," William says, and waits, but nothing. Ma asks Pearl if she wants more tea, asks if Spank was happy to get home, says that Daisy's been good and still, and then she sews on, and the coins on the table catch the sun in this long waiting.

"There's a woman who comes preaching," Pearl finally begins. "Says women are in charge of their own fate."

"Yes, ma'am."

"She comes around, maybe you've seen her? With that stack of magazines?"

"I have."

"She has the preaching in her," Pearl says. "Women's rights and independence. It didn't bother me to listen."

Pearl runs her tongue over the split of her lip and winces. William stares at Ma, but she will not look up from that growing row of stitches.

"Woman says that charity redeems us," Pearl continues, after she has talked herself back into this talking. "That you can leave behind what you've been, have yourself a new beginning, if you turn your heart toward others."

"I guess it." William thinks about the woman and her lookalike girls, how it's the girls she always seems to be leaving in her rush to charity. *How many times have I told you?*

"I thought it would be easy," Pearl says, "getting justice for you and your ma. I thought, one more time, I'll do the business for Kernon. Get the thing and get out and start fresh, a right foot, on my way to my own progress. That's what I thought. My first act of charitable good since the war stole off my husband." Pearl puts a fist to her eye to stop a tear. Ma leaves the needle in the seam to reach for Pearl's hand.

"She had a plan," Ma says. "It was a brave one." She turns the whole dress upside down. Starts in on another row of stitches. Lets Pearl tell.

"It was Jerry who gave me the liquor," Pearl says, collecting herself, "and it was me who got the officer to drinking. A whole night and day of it, 'til he was numb. Socrates Kernon likes his liquor."

"She had him talking," Ma says, "about your brother. She had him show her the ring he had stole. He put it on. Fashioned it on his little finger."

"Your wedding ring, Ma? The officer wore it?" And William tries to picture this—the monster man with the octopus face, wearing Ma's own wedding band, boasting of his murder of Francis.

"Wore it on the tip of his smallest finger," Pearl says, showing William how. "And then he took it off and he left it by the bed and I waited until he was good and numb, and then I took it."

"You took Ma's ring?"

"I did, but he knew it straightaway. Called me a dirty whore, called me worse things."

"How'd he see it, if he was stupored?"

"Not stupored enough, is what I guess."

"He beat her," Ma says. "Beat her so hard, she thought he'd kill her."

"He's a mean man," Pearl says, and she sobs a little, catches herself. "Worst kind of person there is." She has both fists up to her eyes, and Ma's crying, too, she can't help it. Pearl's so pale in the white sun, so bruised, and William's sitting and watching and helpless as Ma reaches across the table for Pearl's hand. They sit like that, and not even Daisy stirs.

"Look what it is," Ma says to William, finally. "Look what Pearl did." And now she reaches into the bosom of her dress, and opens out her hand. The ring is there, in the fizz of sun. *God bless our marriage, Essie.*

"You got the ring back," William says, a bewildered hush.

"I hid it here," Pearl points to her mouth, "between my cheek and gum. Chomped it in and held tight. And not his fist and not his blackjack would take it from me. He couldn't have what he wanted. Not this once."

"But Pearl. . ." William says.

"I'm done with it," she tells him. "Done with the business." She's crying outright, and so is Ma, the ring still there on the palm of her hand, catching the July sun.

Thirty-four

It's Monday, the first of August, and Career comes around early, whistling some tune that floats inside to where Ma and Pearl are sitting in the afternoon light working an old dress into the size and shape of Pearl, talking lost things and second chances, what a woman would do over if she could. They talk the things no sons are meant to hear, and William is upstairs sorting the chunks of coal alongside Francis's bed, the bird feathers and watch fobs, the Schmitt souvenirs, that box the rabbit came home in, the stuff of the pawning and thieving and wanting, when he hears Career's incoming song, though it's Molly who runs to it first. William hears her shout, and when he stands and steps to the window and looks down, he sees her running into the street in a bright pink dress, her orange hair caught up in a cherry-colored bow. She wears her ma's old boots, scruffy and large as two wash pails. She flags her hands in Career's direction, like he already didn't see her collective color. He stops like Career would and plays her a game of penny toss, shows her the way to bend her knees. Molly studies his face—speculating, William is almost sure, on her someday wedding vows. Her small back is swayed and her arms are crossed. She tightens the flop of her bow and takes her place beside her man, suddenly shy with her toss.

"Come on, Daisy," William says and the kid's up and out of her nap in a quick second, bleating and prancing on her padded toes until William reaches down to collect her.

"You're getting too big to be held," he scolds her, kissing the top of her head. She nips him on the ear. She settles. William heads down the stairs and nods goodbye to Ma and Pearl, the bundle of Daisy bleating on him.

"I'll be home," he says. "Right after dark."

"I'm certain of it," Ma says, and when she lifts her hand, Pa's ring effervesces with the sun.

"You're early, ain't you?" William asks Career now. Career finishes his toss and puts his hand on Molly's shoulder. "You practice up some more," he tells her, "and someday you'll outright win."

"Don't you want your penny back?" Molly asks. She touches the place Career's hand just left, tentative, like she's been blessed.

"Not yet," he says. "You keep it for your practice."

"But can I come with you? *Please?*" She shields her eyes from the sun, yanks at that bow, stands there hopeful and curious.

"Not today, Molly. Don't your ma need you?"

"My ma does not." Molly stomps her boot on the street and a cloud of dust bumps up. It leaves a little fog between the ankles of her borrowed boots and that bright pink dress, too short by some.

"You practice your toss, then."

"Why can't I come?"

"William and I have business, is why," Career says. "It can't be helped."

Molly scrunches herself into a probable fit, but now Mrs. May, hanging over the sill of her window, calls Molly in for a piece of fresh pie. "It be the peach pie, ma'am?" Molly asks her, skeptical, and Mrs. May says that it is.

"*Fresh* peach?"

"Ripened," Mrs. May tells her. "You want it or you don't?"

"I guess."

"You come in, then. Leave those boys alone."

"You coming back?" Molly asks, squinting up at Career and at the same time tracing the toe of her ma's boot over a bump in the sunbaked road.

"When my work allows it," Career says, "I will."

"Your work's important, ain't it?"

"I suspect it is."

"You going to be famous?"

"Maybe I will. Now go on. Pie won't get any better."

"Can I keep Daisy for the afternoon?" Molly asks William, but he shakes his head no, will not fall for this girl's stall tactic.

"You want your pie or not, Molly?" Mrs. May calls, leaning further out into the street and stroking that hair on her chin. "Should I be offering it to somebody else?"

"I'm coming," Molly answers and then, looking straight at Career, she says, as if to prove she has marry-able manners, "I'm grateful for the offer, ma'am." She takes a little bow, then folds into a curtsy. "Tomorrow, I'll beat you at toss," she tells Career, slipping that penny into the pink dress's pocket.

"She's so in love with you," William says, as they head off.

"She's nothing but a kid, William," Career says, but he turns back. Looks over his shoulder as Molly bounds up the stoop to Mrs. May's brick house.

They walk a distance before Career tells. They walk the machinery hum, the rubble and the tracks, the honk of a stray goose, the scrapping chase of the three dogs. They take Daisy up into the cool shade of the Preston garden, both of them, Career sucking his pipe and working lookout as Daisy chomps into the crusting heads of the old hydrangea. They crawl back out of the shade and walk up north, past Brandywine and Green and toward the rest of it. It's not until then that Career explains why he's come this time of day, what business it is that he has.

"I had my sit down," he says, a smile breaking above the square line of his jaw.

"Your Mr. Childs?"

Career nods. "Took me aside. Gave me an hour in his office." The sun is coming slantwise and William has to squint. There's light in the black of Career's eyes, a color to his cheeks.

"You're telling me the actual?" William asks, even though he knows that Career wouldn't lie, that he wouldn't be looking as tall as he is now, or taking such long strides.

"He called me in," Career says. "He sat me down. Asked me what's on my mind."

William tries to imagine it—a sit down with Mr. Childs, greatest news editor the city's seen, greatest man, according to some, spying over his half glasses at the best friend William will ever have. He takes a sidelong look at Career in that silver vest of his, that stitched-up charcoal-toned sack jacket. He looks at the tuck of his black hair in that tweedy cap. He looks at the boots with their coat of dust and traction and wonders, *How did Career look to the man?*

"What did you tell him," William asks, "about what you want?" Career gestures for Daisy on her yellow lead, and William hands her over, telling her to be good, to mind that hydrant up ahead, that cab coming.

"Said I want my learning. Said I want my way toward being a proper man."

"You said it just like that?"

"More or less." Daisy skirts the hydrant but makes a dash for the street. Career hauls her back, leans down, talks to her quiet.

"You say anything else?" William asks, when they're going again.

"I told him about the One Thing."

"You confided that?"

167

"Told him I had frugal in me, know the value of holding on."

A mutt comes on, a bluish color with a tusky face. Daisy gets herself into a growling posture. William picks her up, takes on the leash, looks hard at Career, scratches his head. "That's what you said?" he asks. "That you have the frugal in you?" William again tries to conjure it all— Career across the desk from the *Ledger* man. Talking holding on, like a businessman.

"He asked me what I was holding on for. I said I was saving up for books."

"*Books,* you told him?"

"A library's worth. A room gone floor to ceiling with them."

"That's your One Thing?"

Career nods. Daisy squirms. William tells her to be good, and she is.

"All this time it's been?

Career nods again and pulls out his pipe. Sucks some sweetness from it. He touches Daisy on the nose and she bleats. He laughs, looks at William, checks the sun.

"You never said it before."

"I wasn't sure I could."

"But you told it to Mr. Childs."

"It was my sit down. It was my time."

"Best thing for anybody," William says, after they come up on Mt. Vernon, cross it, after he knows there'd be no worth in arguing the fact—

in Career giving his secret up to Childs first, while all this time William waited. "To know and to say." He thinks about Pearl and he thinks about Ma. He thinks about the more he could have done. What saying is and what saying isn't, and what trails get left behind.

"I want to write the news, William," Career says, breaking into William's thoughts. "I want to know it first."

"Man on the scene," William says.

"Man about."

"You'll be good at it, I suppose. The best there is."

"You know how many words is in the dictionary, unabridged?" Career asks.

"I don't."

"One hundred and fourteen thousand, according to the Noah Porter version."

"That a fact?"

"Mr. Childs said it. Took his own *American English* from his shelf and flipped the pages, showed me. Told me to study up on the words when I can, to come talk to him about them."

"From his own shelf, he took it?"

"Said to start my library with it. Said if I might write my stories every night, he might find a reporter to read them. Mentoring me in, he called it. On the presumption that I study up on words."

"An apprentice proper," William says, high with the thought for his friend.

"Something along the lines of it." Career fits the pipe back into his vest pocket and nods, full of the heat of the story. He takes Daisy's lead from William and they walk like that, the three of them, coming into the shadows of the prison. They walk together, side by side, until William claps Career across the back.

"You had yourself one for the books," William says, for Francis's sake.

"I guess I did," Career says. "I guess that's about right."

"My own best friend," William says. "Headed to famous."

William shakes his head and laughs. He whistles a cracked tune on Career's behalf and Daisy gets anxious with it, eager, like dancing. She pulls at her lead, and Career calls her back, but the kid is wanting forward; she's bucking.

"What is it, girl?" William asks, leaning in and stroking the white space between her white ears. "What is it gone wrong?"

Daisy pronounces every word she knows. She points her nose to the falling sun and chatters out, growls, and in the shadow of the prison, at the edge of Twenty-second, William scoops Daisy up into his arms, and she repeats her story, anxious.

"I hear what Daisy hears," William tells Career. "You hear it too?"

Career cocks his head and shuts his eyes. He tilts in the river's direction, toward the sound of a clattering commotion—up west and a little north.

Daisy says it again, whatever it is, and suddenly the boys are running—Daisy in William's arms, then Daisy in Career's, then Daisy down on the street, fast as she can in Molly's yellow necklace. Past the prison they run, over and up and all the way to Parrish street, where a crowd has gathered, kids milling mostly, also their mothers, each of them, maybe two dozen, hovering above the vapors of raw sewage. William's the first to see what has sent the smell up—a hole in the street, a big black darkness.

"What is it?" Career asks, out of breath. He's clapped his hands to his knees and pulls the oxygen back through him. He lets Daisy wander around on that yellow lead. She pulls back from the smell, looks at William to explain, circles close to the hole, then pulls off; the smell's that awful.

"Don't know," William says, equally twisted. "Can't make something of it." He gets down on his hands and his knees and stares into the hole. He looks up at the crowd milling and pointing. The crowd mills and the boys don't play and the mothers with their aprons on don't swat at their sons with their hands. It's like something's come and haunted them to stillness. Like they've seen it but can't say it, whatever it is here, on Parrish.

"It's just that man-hole come off," Career says after a while, pointing to the hole in the street. "Ain't it?"

"Can't be the only thing," William says. "Can't be all the crowd's come for." He studies it again—the haphazard consternation, the hole and the crowd, and the stinking trail of big boot prints—three pairs, headed north. William scoops up Daisy and settles her down into Career's arms.

171

He gets down on his hands and knees again, holds his breath, stares deep into the pit until the smell of it slams down into his lungs, and he has no choice to back off. A boy, no more than six, comes near to give Daisy a pat on the head. He's got slicked-back hair and socks past his boots. He's missing the buttons around his collar.

"They came right out of it," the boy says, before William even asks him.

"Who did?"

The kid shrugs. "Those men there, see 'em?" he points his finger along the trail of the boot treads, toward a cloud of dust, toward another knot of mothers and babies and sons with torn trouser knees. "We was playing when we heard it," the kid says.

"Heard what?" Career asks.

"The tap-tap."

"Coming from the hole?" William tries to straighten the facts.

"That's right. The hole there. We heard the knocking, so we stopped."

"You stopped your playing, is that right?" Career asks, like the reporter he'll be. "For the sound of a tap-tap against the street grate."

"That's what we did," the kid nods stern. " And we asked the Boyer kids to move the lid, because they're the biggest ones of us. Boyer kids are boxers, all three." The kid turns and points to the three who are freckled like the Irish—shoulders up to their ears, big hands.

"So then what?" William asks.

"So then they pushed the lid, the Boyer kids did, and they were there, the three of 'em. One after the other. Climbing out."

"There were three men inside?" Career repeats, getting it straight. "Three men coming up from the hole?"

"That's right. Three of 'em down in. Three of 'em come out. Rose out from the bottom of the earth. Through that hole."

"Came from the sewage?" William asks, straining and seeing nothing but the boot tracks in their journey north, the smell of mud and stink.

"Black as night," the kid says. "All of 'em were. Black in their skin and black with the sewage."

"But what were they doing in the hole?" Career asks. "Did any of them say?"

The boy makes an I-don't-know face.

"They make mention of anything when they come up?" William asks.

"They were stink faced," the boy says. "They were stink faced and didn't say nothing. One of 'em said thank you. Maybe as much."

"Did not," another kid comes around and insists. He's got a blue suit on and a crooked tie. His feet are brown and naked. "None of them said nothing. They just kept walking."

"Said they were working," the other kid says, changing his story. "Said they were working the pipe length."

"Did not," the other kid insists. "Did not. Said nothing but thank you."

"Curious," Career says, and William nods that it is, and he asks Daisy

173

what she thinks, since it was Daisy, after all, who led the chase from the prison, over the thin streets, to here. Daisy with the ears and the nose and the undying knowing, the hope in her, the expectation. William picks her up and he talks into her ear. He places her back down onto the street. Her ears flick fierce and her black eyes fret and then she lays her ears low and stares skyward. William handles her tug and looks up alongside her, Career, too, and now both the boys see what Daisy has seen—that solo flying bird. Not toward the prison, but somewhere north, above the muddy trails.

"You see what it is?" William says to Career, quiet now and cautious.

"I do."

"You see which direction it is flying to?"

"I see it."

"That bird," William says. "That bird knows something."

Career takes off his cap, brushes back his hair, stares up, and slowly nods. He follows the arc of the bird, flying low, near the streets, along the line of stinking treads.

"Jail break," William whispers, the words tremulous.

"I'm concluding like you."

"Three men free. Do you think. . .?"

"I do."

"That maybe they know Pa? Maybe they'd know his story?"

For just a second more, they stand—the two best friends and Daisy, watching the bird flying low, flying north, watching the men disappear.

"If they're jail break they're not going to stop for some questions," Career says.

"I'm sure of it. Still."

"If they're jail break, then they're running for hiding."

"You got the run in you, Daisy?" William leans in and asks the goat, and now he takes off, his arms winged out like that bird of his, the slosh of his feet in Pa's boots, the breeze up into the folds of Francis's trousers. "Come on!" he tells Career, and Career yells out, "I am," and that's how they run, the two of them with the goat in between. Questions to ask, answers they're needing.

Thirty-five

All night they look, but the men are gone. They've run through the streets, north, their boot prints leaving sewage stink until the stink is vanished, too, the stink is vapors. All night the boys walk the alleys and the back behinds, the little trails where no one goes, the nothing lean-tos, where escapees might easily hide. All night making it clear as day that they don't mean the escapees harm. They just have some things to ask. They just have some wondering about Pa.

But the men have left no trace of themselves; they are three who tried and made it. Tomorrow they'll be front-page news. They'll be heroes stood up tall to the silent vault of fat-walled Cherry Hill.

"We still seen what we seen," Career says, tired now, his vest gone ragged.

"We did."

"We seen what's *possible*."

"Possible for them."

"Possible for anybody."

"My Pa's got four more years." William feels it hard against his ribs, this count of time, this missing that he has for his father. He feels it hard that they lost the men, that they didn't get a single question in. Four years forward is four winters and four summers. Four years forward is William eighteen years old. It seems forever from now. Seems like too much hurt and too much caring. Too much responsibility. Too much missing Pa and missing Francis.

"I got a lot more whistle tunes," Career says, into the darkness.

"Pa hears 'em," William says. "I'm sure of it."

"And he'll come out straight and sober," Career says, still looking for the good in William's losses. "And your Ma will have her wedding band. And that's thanks to you, William."

"That's thanks to Pearl."

"To you and to Pearl."

The night is shadow; the moon is thin. They've made their way all the way back to Preston Retreat, and there are babies crying through windows. William wonders, for a moment, if the lookalikes are near. Daisy gives a tug toward the bushes.

"Let's give her a good chew or two," Career says.

"Ma will be anxious."

"Just a little chew," Career says, and William knows it's right and proper. A good goat deserving a good meal. They stand and let Daisy do the business of hers. They stand in dark, listening. Poor mothers up there and their poor little babies. The machines all around, a city of futures.

"You going to go to the *Ledger*," William asks, "and report on it?"

"I will."

"You going to tell them what we saw?"

"Every bit of it," Career says. "None exaggerated."

"Your Mr. Childs will like that."

"I reckon he will."

"Your Roast-Beef will be jealous."

"He'll get his story someday."

"But this one's yours," William says. "This is your bit of famous. Prison breaks like that don't happen. Except that Francis said it would. Francis. He knew something good would come."

"The lucky Quinns," Career says.

Daisy returns of her own accord, nudges up against William's trousers. He picks her up and she nips his ear. She runs her tongue along his jawbone.

"You're getting famous, too," Career says, and they're walking again, crossing the tracks, headed south, to the next far corner. "You and your talent for creatures."

"It ain't nothing."

"It's something fair," Career says. "And honest. It's what you can do, and you do it."

"It ain't hard."

"You make things *right,*" Career says. "Most people can't do it."

They walk some more without talking. William thinks on it, wonders if it's true. Wonders if fair and honest amounts to something, if fair and honest can see him and his Ma through, and Pearl, too, and Career, always, and Pa, in the right now and in the later. He wonders what Francis would think if he could see him now. What he would say. What he would think. What he would promise.

"Turning for home," Career says, when the reach corner at Carleton. He puts his hand out in the dark to tap William's shoulder. He gives Daisy a little between-the-ears nudge.

"I'll be looking for you in tomorrow's *Ledger*," William says.

"You'll see me," Career says. "That's a good-for promise."

"You be there, and we'll throw you a feast," William says. "Ma and Pearl and Mrs. May. We'll even invite your Molly."

"Molly's just a kid," Career says, but even in the dark William sees him smiling.

LOCAL AFFAIRS.

ESCAPE FROM THE EASTERN PENITENTIARY—PRISONERS MAKE THEIR WAY OUT THROUGH A SMALL CULVERT—An escape from the Eastern Penitentiary has generally been regarded as among the impossible things. The constant watchfulness that is exercised, the manner in which the convicts are confined, and the difficulty in procuring the necessary aids to flight, supposing the plan looked to a scaling of walls, all tended to create that belief. No one, not even those who have been the longest connected with the Penitentiary as managers or keepers, had the least idea that a small culvert used for drainage would be the means of facilitating escape.

Three of the convicts, all colored men, two of whom had been sent from one of the interior counties for horse stealing, the other a convict, whose good conduct had been won upon the confidence of the warden and keepers, that he was employed as a runner on one of the corridors, were enabled to effect their enlargement on Monday afternoon under these circumstances. Two of the fugitives were engaged in whitewashing the cells and otherwise purifying them, and discovering the grating over the opening into the culvert, they watched an opportunity when the overseer was momentarily away, and lifting the plate made their way down to the culvert followed by the runner, who had doubtless been spoken to on the subject of it.

The men were missed very soon afterwards, but until a condition of the grating was discovered, it was not thought they had any intention of leaving the Penitentiary. Now it was apparent to the keepers that they had descended into the culvert, but none supposed they would be able to reach the street. It was known that when the Coates street culvert was built, a gate had been placed at the mouth of the Penitentiary culvert, to prevent the escape of prisoners, and this was depended upon the check their flight in that direction. They were, however, able to remove it, and to make their way into the new culvert on Corinthian avenue, along which they passed as far as Parrish street. At this point, a crack in the plate covering the man-hole sent a ray of light through to the imprisoned men, and they began to knock against the plate. That noise was heard by some boys playing in the street, and they assisted to raise the cover.

The story of the men was that they had been sent into the culvert to clean it, and having been almost suffocated with foul air, they wanted to get out. Their story was believed, they were assisted out and made their escape. The officers of the Penitentiary had not thought of the Corinthian avenue culvert, not supposing there could be a passage from the drainage culvert of the Penitentiary to it. Nor did they believe it possible the men could go safely through the small culvert, which is said to be but two and a half feet in diameter and several hundred feet long. The fugitives are named Thomas Dare and John and William Thomas. They had been sentenced to long terms for horse-stealing. They had behaved very well, and for that reason had been put to whitewashing.

Afterword

Dr. Radway's Sarsaparilla Resolvent is a story that revives many of the places and people that made late 19th century Philadelphia so spectacular. Matthias Baldwin was indeed a master locomotive designer and industrialist (and lover of orchids), and Bush Hill (now known as the Spring Garden area) throbbed with his machine works. George Childs was the beloved *Public Ledger* editor who daily brought young men into his office to give them advice on life—and, often, books and study money. Eastern State Penitentiary (called Cherry Hill back then by locals) was one of the most talked-about prison systems in the world; even Charles Dickens came to have a look in the early 19th century. Max Schmitt competed in the race that is reported in this novel, and Thomas Eakins was on hand to paint the scene. You could buy Dr. Radway's Sarsaparilla Resolvent in Manayunk and you could purchase New Jersey produce at the Market on 12th Street. An Officer Socrates Kernon did murder a Francis Quinn. The accident at the Baldwin Works happened just as it unfolds here, with the very same people involved, and so did the August prison break. Animals were, indeed, being lost and found, providing a good (if unreliable) wage to young people like William.

To write this story I roamed my city. I spent time (not *that* kind of time) at the Penitentiary. With my father at my side, I took a walking tour of vanished sites with Harry Kyriakodis, a local historian who also kindly sent me many old, instructive maps and photographs. I sat quietly in the reading room of the Historical Society of Pennsylvania, looking through old picture books and guides, learning the cost of transportation and the routes the trains and horse-drawn trolleys took, thumbing through the Samuel B. Fales collection of Union Volunteer Refreshment Saloon papers, finding (at long last) an image of the Norris House. I first discovered Preston Retreat, the obstetric hospital once located on Hamilton above 20th Street, in an 1868 Philadelphia guidebook. This extraordinary institution, founded by Revolutionary-era physician Dr. Jonas Preston, had been created especially for poor mothers of Philadelphia—all poor mothers, of every "class or racial distinction"—and I knew at once that it would have a place in my novel, because that's what historical novels do: they bring missing places back to life.

I read. I read a lot. I read Paul Kahan's *Eastern State Penitentiary: a History*, Norman Johnston's *Eastern State Penitentiary: Crucible of Good Intentions*, and John K. Brown's *The Baldwin Locomotive Works, 1831-1915: a Study in American Industrial Practice*. I read a tiny pamphlet on the life of Matthias W. Baldwin by a man named Ralph Kelly. I read Philadelphia history books, Philadelphia biographies, Philadelphia tomes. I read (as all lovers of history and cities do) the old newspapers—*The New York Times*, the *Public Ledger*, *The Philadelphia Inquirer*. I read not just for the front-page tales—the drownings, the horrors, the inventions,

186

the politics, the crimes, the trials, the accidents at Baldwin Locomotive Works, the funeral of Matthias Baldwin—but for the fabulous provocations that appeared on the pages of the various classifieds. I found my oddball collection of medicines—E.F. Kunkel's Bitter Wine of Iron, Alburger's Celebrated Berman Bitters, Dr. Van Dyke's cure—in the classifieds, not to mention Dr. Radway and his outrageous claims. I found the things that Francis would steal, the E. Burthey Cream Drops, the florist known as Bisele's, the Phasmatrope. I found, most importantly, those many Lost and Found ads that provided William with his identity and career as a gentle soul who could coax lost animals back to their proper homes, and be rewarded for his talents. All newspaper articles or classified ads in this novel were excerpted from the actual news stories of the day—from both the *Public Ledger* and *The Philadelphia Inquirer.* Spellings of places and things are also reflective of the period itself.

My friend Adam Levine, the Philadelphia Water Department historian, answered questions when I asked. Karen Young, the director of the Fairmount Water Works Interpretive Center, and Stacey Swigart, Curator of Collections for Please Touch Museum, offered encouragement. Amy Rennert and Robyn Russell read the novel early on, and I am grateful. Micah Kleit of Temple University Press opened a door. Quinn Colter, a young reader and writer, took a careful and deeply appreciated sweep through the manuscript. Gary Kramer, publicist supreme and friend, has stood by. Elizabeth Parks gave the pages form, and class. Steve Parks

187

of New City Community Press read at once and has been, ever since, an enthusiastic partner in this endeavor. He understood why William's story meant so much to me. He believed, as I believe, in the power of stories such as these to return a lost era to a city.

Dr. Radway's Sarsaparilla Resolvent represents my third bookish collaboration with my husband, my own William, who is, among other things, a remarkable illustrator. I wanted this story to live in many dimensions. His art and his talent made that possible.

Finally, my thanks to the team at Egmont USA for publishing *Dangerous Neighbors*, my Centennial Philadelphia novel, where William and those twins first appear in print. And many thanks to Temple University Press for *Flow: The Life and Times of Philadelphia's Schuylkill River*, where I first wrote about the river and city that continue to inspire me.

About the Author

Beth Kephart, a National Book Award finalist, is the author of fifteen books, including the BookSense pick *Ghosts In The Garden*; *Flow: The Life And Times Of Philadelphia's Schuylkill River*; the IndieBound Picks *The Heart Is Not A Size* and *Dangerous Neighbors*; and the critically acclaimed novels for young adults *Undercover, House Of Dance, Nothing But Ghosts, You Are My Only*, and *Small Damages*. Her book about the making of memoir, *Handling The Truth*, will be released by Gotham in 2013.

Kephart's acclaimed short story, "The Longest Distance," appears in the May 2009 HarperTeen anthology, *No Such Thing As The Real World*. She is a winner of the Pennsylvania Council on the Arts fiction grant, a National Endowment for the Arts grant, a Leeway grant, a Pew Fellowships in the Arts grant, and the Speakeasy Poetry Prize, among other honors. Kephart's essays are frequently anthologized, she has judged numerous competitions, and she has taught workshops to all ages at many institutions. Kephart teaches creative nonfiction at the University of Pennsylvania and served as the inaugural readergirlz author in residence. Her work has been translated into fifteen languages.

Kephart is the strategic writing partner in the award-winning marketing communications firm, Fusion. She has written for the *Philadelphia*

Inquirer, New York Times Book Review, Chicago Tribune, Shelf Awareness, and *Publishing Perspectives* and is represented by Amy Rennert of The Amy Rennert Agency.

Please visit her blog, www.beth-kephart.blogspot.com, which was voted a top author blogs in 2009 and 2011 during Book Blogger Appreciation Week.

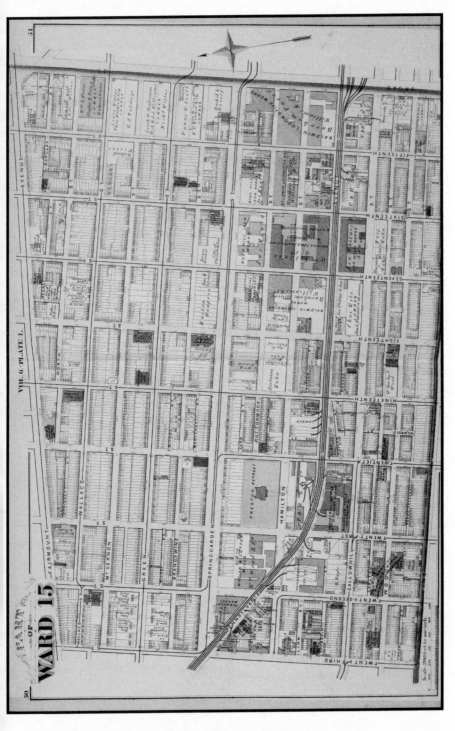